Kimchi & Calamari

Kimchi & Calamari

Not So Happy Birthday to Me

You wake up and you're fourteen. The world is your supersized soda waiting to be guzzled, right? Wrong. My birthday tasted more like Coke that went flat.

Make that flat Coke with cookie crumbs from my little sister's backwash.

Not that I *planned* on a lousy birthday. After all, I'm Joseph Calderaro, eighth-grade optimist. The bag of barbecue chips is always half full in my mind. As I searched for my Yankees T-shirt that morning, I tapped out my favorite band tune with my drumsticks. I was ready to hit the halls of Johansen Middle School bursting with I'm-all-that attitude. I couldn't wait to hear "Happy Birthday to Joseph" chants from cute girls in the hallway between classes. And of course, I expected to uphold my family's tradition of gorging on my favorite dinner. Fried calamari. Eggplant Parmesan. Chocolate cake with gobs of cannoli frosting. Even the whines from Gina and Sophie couldn't ruin that meal.

Little did I know that my burned Pop-Tart breakfast would be a sign of trouble ahead. Or that the day's events would spiral downward, just like that pastry— from strawberry frosted and gooey good to black-on-the-bottom and smoking bad.

I should've known better, what with all the comic books I've read: villains wreak havoc when you least expect it. In this case, the villain struck during second period. I was tilting my desk chair back, feeling mighty proud of the "To Burn or Not to Burn" project I'd turned in, analyzing a constitutional amendment against flag desecration. I'd surrounded the poster's edges with flag toothpicks, and I'd taped power quotes from two Supreme Court justices.

With ten minutes left in the period, Mrs. Peroutka started lecturing about the upcoming unit: immigration.

I was still feeling thirsty and sweaty from the mile run in gym, never mind sleep deprived from gluing toothpicks until eleven thirty last night. Nothing Mrs. Peroutka said was keeping my attention, especially with that warm breeze rattling through the blinds.

Nothing, that is, until she dropped a slab of cement on my head. It came in the form of a handout, but trust me, it caused quite the emotional concussion.

"I have an assignment for you," she announced, with a diabolical twinkle in her eye.

As soon as I read the top line of the paper, my heart started racing like I was back on the track running.

Tracing Your Past: A Heritage Essay

"Before we discuss the assignment, I'd like you to consider this: Who are your ancestors?" she asked.

Next to me, fellow drummer Steve Nestor popped his arm straight up. "Dead people with your same last name?"

Robyn Carleton chuckled in the back row. She appreciates all jokes, especially mine.

"Indeed, our ancestors are dead *and* related," Mrs. Peroutka replied, "but they are much more than that. Each one of your families owns a patch on America's collective immigrant quilt: the dreams and the struggles of your kin who came before you. Ancestors are your

3

personal link to yesterday."

Ugh. Faces around the room looked pained. Honestly, who gives eighth graders an essay in May? Maybe fall, or even January, when you're guaranteed at least one snow day. But a May essay is a low blow, what with June around the corner, the month in which we break out of the middle-school penitentiary forever.

Mrs. Peroutka droned on, her voice deep like a narrator on the History Channel. Then she gave us the dirty details. Required words: fifteen hundred. Double-spaced. Blah blah blah. She stood poised by the chalkboard, her hand clutching a pen in midair like the Statue of Liberty, and rambled on about digging out old photos and interviewing family members. But I tuned out right after hearing "your ancestors." I didn't know diddly about my ancestors.

Right before the bell rang, Mrs. Peroutka told us the essay was part of a Celebrating Your Heritage campaign that had kids across America tracing their lineages back to over 175 countries.

"Like that's supposed to make us want to join hands with other eighth graders from sea to shining sea," Steve whispered to me.

After class I waited at the lockers for my buddy Nash, and we walked to the cafeteria together. I told him this

4

birthday felt as lousy as the woodwinds playing "Rock with Bach." Nash is in band too—he plays trumpet—so he totally got what I meant.

"I can't believe we have to do a social studies essay in May," I complained.

He groaned. "How many words?"

"Fifteen hundred."

Nash uses the bazooka technique for writing papers. He strings together all these run-on sentences that stretch longer than a wad of bubblegum—just to hit the required word count.

"What kind of teacher serves up a paper after a project?" Nash said, shaking his head.

I told him the topic of the essay was part of the problem too. "You know what I wanted to tell Mrs. Peroutka? I don't need fifteen hundred words. Two will wrap it up nicely: I'm adopted."

As soon as I sat down at the lunch table, more bad fortune revealed itself from under the plastic wrap. Mom had mixed up my sandwich with Gina's. I was stuck with peanut butter and banana slices, a hideous combo surely created to make POWs talk.

Nash caught my disgusted look and stared down at my sandwich. "Yuck. That looks nasty. Poor you."

"So much for special treatment on my birthday," I said.

He passed me some pretzels. "Your lunch might stink, but at least your mom's making your favorite dinner, right?"

I nodded, thinking about Mom in the kitchen slicing and salting eggplant and sprinkling cheese. She'd taken a day off from the hair salon to shop and cook.

I shoved the sandwich back in the bag and bit into a pretzel. "You're right, Nash. I won't let old Peroutka be the Grinch who steals my birthday. So come over tonight ready for one grandioso Calderaro feast."

The Evil Eye

Bread crumbs come in regular or Italian. So do suits, though Dad says the Italian ones fit better across his thick shoulders. And I know Mom wouldn't dare make her chicken cacciatore with anything but Italian plum tomatoes. But who knew that jewelry was made especially for natives of the boot-shaped country? And why should I, of all people, care about that?

"I'm so stuffed that eggplant Parmesan is coming out my pores," I said to Nash as we waited for Mom to finish slicing the cake. Not that second helpings of dinner would stop me from digging into dessert. Nash can eat me under the table, and he'd still fit in an envelope. Me, from the moment I arrived from Korea, I was nicknamed Buddha Baby. The name fit then and it still does, though I'm not really fat—just stocky with a barrel chest and stubby arms and legs.

"Mommy said for us to get the presents," Sophie said to Gina in what Mom calls her "eight-year-old Mussolini voice." My twin sisters scooted out from behind the kitchen table with Frazer, our plump old boxer, trotting behind them. They were back in a flash, carrying boxes they could barely hold. One fell out of Gina's arms and she quickly picked it up, though she didn't notice the bow sticking to her knee.

But Nash and I did, and we laughed. He's used to my wacky family. Pete Nash moved to Nutley in first grade. Back then kids called him Nash Potato because he brought mashed potatoes and gravy in a thermos for lunch all the time. He took some brutal teasing about that thermos, but he kept showing up with it anyway. Which I can understand because his mom's mashed potatoes taste mighty delicious.

"Wait! Don't open any presents until you read your you-know-what, Joseph," Mom said. "For good luck. It's under your plate as usual."

Rats. I thought Mom forgot about that weird horoscope tradition. I lifted my plate and unfolded the clipped newspaper page.

> Taurus: Understand that you are entering a new
> chasm of change. Any benefits or gains you
> make this new year may not be obvious at first,
> though the pain is.

I frowned after I read it. Funny thing was, I *did* feel different. And not just because my voice was starting to crack and I was getting a hairy-creature-in-puberty look. Melodramatic "Who am I?" questions kept popping into my mind all afternoon. Probably because of that rotten essay assignment.

Mom must have noticed my expression. "Don't read bad into it, Joseph. Change can be good. Yesterday I turned a washed-out brunette into a stunning blonde, and she was thrilled with *that* change."

"Can we eat our cake now? I'm starving!" Gina whined.

"Yuck. Cannoli frosting," Sophie groaned.

"It's Joseph's birthday, remember?" Dad said, sipping his coffee. "Go ahead and open your presents, son."

I started ripping through shiny paper and shouting

out the "Wow, you shouldn't have!" comments that parents get all gushy about. And I *did* like my gifts, especially the Spider-Man alarm clock that I'd been eyeing at the mall. Spider-Man is The Man, and my hero. I love how his alias, Peter Parker, forgets stuff and blabs dumb comments to girls like the rest of us. But in the end he always delivers the spider goods. Which is to say he saves the world, tells a joke or two, and beats the sinister snot out of his archenemy, Venom.

Nash likes comic book heroes too, though his favorite is Wolverine, the furry X-Man with retractable claws. Not that we discuss this stuff in school. Being known as a comic book dork is worse than wearing jeans that fit right, or a ski hat with a giant pom-pom.

The next gift was a video game from Mom and Dad, the very one I was hoping for. I guess writing "Get Joseph a video game" in washable marker across Mom's hairstylist station mirror did the trick. Then Gina and Sophie gave me a huge bag of peanut M&M's, and Nash gave me a joke book.

"Without further ado, let's hit the game controls," I told Nash after my last forkful of cake.

But Dad stopped us. "Wait a second, Joseph. Mom and I have one more present for you."

"I'll get it, Vinny." Mom walked into the laundry room

and returned with a small box.

"What is it? What is it?" Gina jumped in her chair.

My fingers ripped through the wrapping paper. I opened the box and then I saw it: a gold chain with a tiny gold horn, shaped like an antler.

I almost blurted out, "What the heck is this thing?" when I remembered how Dad wears something like this all the time. It's on the same chain as his crucifix, and it bops up and down when he's doing push-ups. And the last time we visited our relatives in Florida, I noticed Uncle Biaggio had one on when he went swimming.

"It's a *corno*. A goat horn, Joseph. Italian men wear it for good luck. Legend says that it protects against the *malocchio*. You know, the evil eye. Satan's work." Mom narrowed her eyes like she always does when she talks about warding off dark spirits.

Nash looked at Mom like she was an exorcist. Which Mom sort of thinks she is. She's always talking about how the *malocchio* comes when people get cocky, causing others to cast jealous, bad luck glances. She talks about it with this doubting grin like she's way past believing a silly superstition that started in Italy hundreds of years ago, but we all know she buys into it. At least a little.

I looked over at Dad. His bald head beamed from the

fluorescent lamp, and he was grinning like he does when he finishes reading one of those classics. "I got a *corno* from Grandpa Calderaro the year I turned fourteen. I don't know about warding off dark spirits, but it means you're on your way. Growing up. Wear it and be proud."

"Try it on," Mom said.

"Yeah, put it on, Joseph." Dad leaned back in his chair proudly, the way the Pope does after Easter mass.

Put it on? No way. I sat there, speechless, looking down at the frosting flower on Mom's piece of cake. I didn't know *what* to say. Boy, was I glad that Nash was a best friend who wouldn't blab my incriminating moments to others.

"I'll help you." Gina picked up the chain and tried to put it around my neck.

I put my hand out. "Stop, Gina." I stuck the *corno* back in the box.

"What's wrong?" Dad looked confused.

"My neck's hot," I said, rubbing it, and thinking what a nightmare it would be to get caught wearing this in the locker room. Guys at school would think a goat horn looked even weirder than the smiley face boxers Chuck Beski wore last week. And if they did know about the *corno*, that probably meant they were Italian, so they'd sure wonder why it was hanging around *my* Korean neck.

"What, you don't like it?" Dad asked.

"I didn't say that."

"Well you might as well have," he replied. Almost on cue, the vein near Dad's forehead started pulsing in a one-stroke pattern like drum rudiments. *Bum, bum, bum. Bum, bum, bum.* That happens whenever he's upset. We call it his Mad Meter. Dad has his own window-washing business, and one time this snotty rich lady tried to pay him less than what she owed. That got the Mad Meter pulsing for hours.

I could tell Nash felt funny being caught in a Calderaro clash because he started looking around the kitchen, as if scrubbing the crusted sauce pot suddenly sounded appealing.

Mom noticed the Mad Meter too, so she tried to left turn out of the topic. "Pete, do Irish people have any special jewelry?" she asked.

Nash shrugged. "My mom wears a Saint Brigid's cross that's made out of rope, and my sister, Nancy, got a Saint Anthony medal when she graduated from high school."

"He's the patron saint for lost things," Mom said, smiling at Nash. "Italians love him too."

Nash nodded. "Nancy's always losing her car keys."

Sophie picked up the chain and frowned. "I don't like the *corno* either, Daddy. We saw a movie in school about how mean people rip the tusks off elephants. My teacher said the people who buy the tusks make everything worse."

"I think you watch too many movies in school," Dad snapped. "What happened to books?"

"Down with animal cruelty! From now on, I'm a vegetarian," Sophie declared.

I looked over at Dad's forehead. *Bum, bum, bum.* The Mad Meter synchronized better than our sixth-grade drummers.

Funny thing was, when I looked at the *corno*, it reminded me of school too. How I had nothing to write for that dumb ancestry essay.

Then Gina joined in the cause. She's always a me-too kid around Sophie. "Don't wear that horn, Joseph. Everyone has to stop hurting elephants and goats!" She banged the gift box against the table, nearly knocking into her cake plate.

Gina's face was so serious I couldn't control myself. I burst out laughing. Even Nash laughed.

But Dad didn't. The Mad Meter had stopped, and now he looked sad. "It's not a real goat horn. See what you've started, Joseph? A little gratitude would have been nice."

"I am thankful, it's just that I'm not . . ." I stopped myself. This wasn't the time or place, as Mom likes to say.

"You're not *what*?" Dad asked.

I didn't answer.

Dad shook his head. Then he put his mug and cake, untouched, in the sink and walked out of the kitchen.

"Mr. Calderaro's not big on dessert," Mom said to Nash. As if that explained everything.

I felt rotten. Worse than any nasty virus you could get from the *malocchio*.

Niente per Niente

Mrs. Nash's van had just pulled up. Mom was standing in the driveway giving her leftover cake and talking. The sky was brilliant blue that night, so blue it almost looked fake, like pool water.

I walked Nash out to the van with Frazer following us. We'd played my new video game for an hour, but we'd hardly spoken. Ever since that goat horn appeared, I'd been in a bad mood and my stomach hurt. The triple whammy effect of the *malocchio*, overeating, and lactose intolerance.

Mom was telling Mrs. Nash how to get gum off a

couch cushion, so I hopped in the back of the van with Nash while they talked.

"Out of here, you smelly beast," I shouted as Frazer jumped in, but it was too late. He wedged his thick brown butt on my lap and rested his snout on Nash, who started rubbing his ears.

"Sorry you had to hear my dad popping his buttons over that goat horn," I said.

"Your dad's not as bad as my mom. Remember how nutty she got last year when I started getting migraines? She still won't let me play hockey."

Nash's mom is a nurse. What's that saying about too much information being dangerous? I've seen her lose it when she catches him doing something she thinks could cause a migraine. It's not pretty.

"Wearing that *corno* seems so dumb. I'm not Italian. Wouldn't you feel weird if you had to wear a French beret?" I asked Nash.

He scrunched up his freckled face. "Even a French kid would feel weird wearing a beret in middle school. Could you talk to your dad about it?"

"You know my dad. He's Mr. Italiano, always playing Tony Bennett songs and retelling tales from Tuscany. He'll get all mad or sad. That's why I'm in deep doo-doo over this essay. All I know is that my birth relatives put my diapered butt on an airplane to the USA. End of paper."

Nash's eyes widened. "I'm on the computer a lot since I can't play sports now. I could help you search the Internet to find out about the place where you're from in Korea. My uncle traced his genealogy all the way back to this Irish rebel who escaped from a British prison in Belfast in 1912."

"Really?"

"I swear. And he did all his research online."

Hmm. Our family computer wasn't even hooked up to the Internet. And I sure didn't want to be flashing this touchy-feely personal stuff on a screen at the library, especially since the big-mouth reference librarian was one of my mom's regular customers. One time I was there researching the digestive system for a health project, and the next day she asked Mom if I had a nervous stomach. Talk about privacy.

Besides, hunting for my Korean ancestors online might be easier than asking my parents. Dad got testy over a goat horn. And Mom, well, she'd talk about my adoption, but all talk would eventually lead to tears—that's just the way she is. And I don't like making her cry.

"Let me think about it," I said as Mrs. Nash opened the van door. I grabbed Frazer's collar and followed

Mom inside, wondering what just a click of the mouse might reveal about me.

Later that night I lay in bed, looking up at the glow-in-the-dark constellations on the ceiling. Dad stuck them there the day I first rode a two-wheeler. Most of the Big and Little Dippers' stars had fallen off, but Pegasus was still glowing bright.

I kept thinking about the essay. The *corno*. The birthday brawl. And back to that essay. Nash's idea to research Korea online might help me get it done. But did I really need that?

I'd exaggerated a little when I talked to Nash. Mom and Dad haven't exactly engaged in a cloak-and-dagger adoption conspiracy. Mom loved to tell my story, and Dad always hung around listening.

"Time to remember that magical night you came into our lives," Mom would announce when I was little, as she tucked me under my spaceship comforter.

"Once upon a time, Mommy and Daddy wanted a baby to love," she said, rubbing my head. "A wonderful baby who would make us laugh and cry with joy.

"Meanwhile, in Korea, a special mommy was growing you in her tummy, but she couldn't care for a baby. Still, she loved you so much that she did something very hard.

She allowed you to travel all the way to America, to be Mommy and Daddy's little boy. And that is how we became the Calderaro family." Mom always smiled when she said that last line.

Sometimes Mom would describe the stormy night when I arrived at JFK Airport. It was the Saturday after Thanksgiving, and she said Dad was so excited, waiting for the plane, that he passed out plastic cups of champagne to strangers walking by.

"The flight was delayed two hours because of the weather, and you can't imagine how worried we were," Mom said.

Mom has this Italian saying, *niente per niente*, meaning you have to give to get. And when she bargains, she makes sure everybody benefits. That night she struck a deal with San Guiseppe, or Saint Joseph, the patron saint of families.

"I promised that if your plane landed safely, I would toss more money in the church basket for the rest of my life and put his statue smack dab in the middle of my garden. And as you know, he's stood guard in between the geraniums and begonias for fourteen years."

Mom said that when we got home from the airport, I was so hungry I drank two bottles of soy milk. The adoption agency recommended soy milk, and they were right.

I still get the runs from cow's milk.

"The rate you gulped those bottles down, I swear you could've been listed in the *Guinness Book of Records*," Dad always added with a grin. That's the only part of the adoption story he told, even if he listened to Mom's every word, every time.

What my parents never told me is what I call the MBA piece. Me Before America. Maybe because, in my parents' minds, my life started presto, the night Mom and Saint Joseph struck a deal and that 747 touched down on the runway safely.

In third grade, when we had to trace our family tree for homework, Mom told me my Korean name: Duk-kee. That was the name my birth mother gave me. Park was added by the adoption agency. Other than that, I don't know a darn thing about MBA.

Right before I dozed off, Mom came in. She sat at the edge of my bed and smiled.

"Dinner got four stars," I said, and her face lit up. She likes it when I rave about her cooking. "Is Dad still mad?"

"He's not really mad. He just felt hurt that you didn't like our gift. You know how big he is on family tradition," she said, rubbing my head.

"Sorry, Mom. I would just feel funny wearing that *corno*."

"We should've known no teenage boy in Nutley, New Jersey, would be thrilled about a goat horn." She leaned over and kissed me good night.

Staring up at those neon stars got me thinking about Korea. What it looked like and what fourteen-year-olds did there on their birthday. If they fought with their dads and if they had lousy essays to write too. Korea felt so far away. As far as another galaxy. Too far even for the *malocchio* to reach.

The Mona Lisa of Middle School

The next morning I stuck the *corno* way in the back of my socks-and-underwear drawer. Out of sight, out of mind, right? I put that essay out of my mind too, at least for a little while. Today was Friday, alleluia! And the best part about Friday, besides just being Friday, was having Life Skills. That's the politically correct name our school gives sewing and cooking class. It's required for eighth graders. When the teachers and the girls aren't around, the guys call it Sissy Skills, though secretly it's kind of fun.

But the best part about Life Skills, besides eating

gooey, straight-from-the-oven chocolate chip cookies at nine A.M., was seeing my crush, Kelly Gerken.

For weeks I'd been gearing up to ask Kelly if she wanted to go to the movies with me. That's how smart middle-school kids do it. We act like it's the *movie* we're interested in. That way, if the girl says no, we tell ourselves she just didn't want to see that particular flick. My plan was first to ask Kelly how softball was going, since she's the team captain and star pitcher. Then I'd lead into the invite.

Of course, going to the movies would be just the start. Every eighth-grade guy knew the Farewell Formal coming up next month could be the grand finale of middle school or the end-of-year disaster, depending on who you asked and what she said.

I walked into Life Skills and headed straight to the storage closet to get my pillow. The sewing project we'd been working on for a month counted double for our grade. My patchwork pillow needed some tender loving care: the seams didn't match, and the stitching between patches zigzagged like jack-o'-lantern teeth.

Lewis Knight gave me a forced nod as we both reached for our pillows. He's the goalie who made the freshman soccer team long before most of us knew what *varsity* meant. Dad washes his family's windows. When I told him how cocky Lewis was, he said Lewis sounded like a chip off his old man's blockhead. Dad always botches clichés like that. Sometimes his mixed-up sayings are dumb, but other times he cracks us both up.

I sat down at my assigned station, flipped the switch on the sewing machine, and peeked over at Kelly. She had finished sewing all her patches and was already pinning them to the liner. Meanwhile the rest of us were still trying to get the hang of threading the machine needle and catching the bobbin thread before it fell and unraveled across the floor.

Within minutes the Life Skills classroom was humming like a tenor sewing-machine orchestra. My cue to get Kelly's attention.

Think, Joseph, something witty.

My friends say I never shut up and yet there I was, a poet out of words. An iPod without a Play button.

Finally, it hit me.

"Hey, Kelly, guess which local pop-culture icon turned fourteen yesterday? Here's a hint: it's not a movie star or Mrs. Randall." I spoke loudly over the gunning sewing machines, knowing Mrs. Randall was listening too.

"Hmm, let me guess. Joseph Calderaro?" Kelly opened her green, glittery eyes wide, like she had no idea.

I nodded, pretending to be surprised. "How'd you know?"

"Happy belated birthday, Joseph," Mrs. Randall said as she passed my sewing station. She's one of those easygoing teachers who doesn't mind if we talk, as long as we get our work done.

"Mrs. Randall, do you know what they call an explosion in a kitchen in France?"

She shook her head. "What?"

"Linoleum Blownaparte."

"Cute, Joseph," she said, smiling. "Now don't forget to adjust your thread tension."

I lowered the dial from three to one and looked over at Kelly. She was smiling back at me. Directly at me.

"Yeah, happy late birthday," Kelly said, flashing a twenty-four-karat-gold grin.

God, she was perfect. Even her hair, what with how it was flipped back with silver clips like the stanchions on the Verrazano Bridge.

Last year our art teacher told us that Mona Lisa has been gazed upon more than any other woman in the history of the world. Personally, I don't think she's much to look at, what with that foot-long forehead and her lips clamped shut like she's got dental problems. Kelly, on the other hand, has two straight rows of pearls in her mouth.

"So where'd you spend the day commemorating your birth, at a nudist colony?" Robyn Carleton shouted from her sewing station.

I wished I could tell her that I was having a humongous birthday bash this weekend, just so I could invite Kelly.

"I skipped the party this year," I said. "All those flashing cameras from the paparazzi hurt my eyes."

Then Kelly told the whole class that she was having a retro-disco party when she turned fourteen in August. "I've got fifty names on the invite list, and I've barely begun," she said, just as Rhonda Gardner walked over to her, whispered something, and pointed to Lewis.

My friend Frankie Marquette told me that I was setting myself up for rejection by liking Kelly. And not just because she's athletic and pretty, though she is *very* athletic and pretty. Kelly is rich, too. Her dad owns a bunch of restaurants in central Jersey. Mom and Dad celebrated their twentieth wedding anniversary at one of the Gerkens' seafood restaurants last winter. Mom said the salmon was melt-in-your-mouth tender, but Dad complained that the waiters buzzed around the table like nervous bees.

I think Frankie completely underestimates the power of humor. He thinks you impress girls with how many push-ups you do in gym or by wearing hundred-dollar jeans that look a hundred years old. Me? I say a guy can get a girl interested by making her laugh.

Five minutes left in the period and my heart was pounding *boom-ba-ba-boom* like a bass drum. I had to time my every move so that I'd leave just as Kelly did. A Saturday matinee date was at stake.

The God of Perfect Timing must like drummers. Kelly and I walked out of class side by side.

"Hey, I hear you're playing an amazon softball team today," I said, holding the door open for her.

She nodded. "Paterson won the division title for the past two years. But right now we've got the best record in the league."

We passed the science labs and headed to the lockers. Kelly told me she'd been taking private pitching lessons all spring. "Paterson has an awesome hitter who's six feet tall. I hope all this extra coaching helps me strike out that giant."

My mind was racing, ready to pop the question. I even had this dumb baseball riddle from Gina to tell her. But I had to be quick. English class was next, way down the hall.

"Hey, Kelly, I was wondering—"

Wham! Who wedged right between us but Lewis. He played like I was the Invisible Man and he was the suave superhero, yakking it up with my girl Kelly. And that was it. Advantage came and went for the birthday boy.

The Emperor with No Clothes

opened my bedroom door early Saturday to find Gina standing there with her lips curved in a horse-shoe.

"Eeyore and I are not having a good morning," she grumbled. Her stuffed donkey was tucked under her arm.

"Whatsamatta?"

"Sophie's watching 'Monster Bashville,' and she knows it scares me," Gina cried as she pushed her glasses back against her nose. "She is *not* nice."

"Don't be scared. You know those mangy-looking puppets aren't real."

"They're creepy. Sophie always gets her way. She's so mean!"

Besides their long brown hair and hiccups, my sisters are as twinnish as tiramasu and tortellini. Since the first time Sophie flung a spoonful of yogurt ten feet from her high chair, we knew she would grow up to be a win-at-all-cost woman warrior. Gina, on the other hand, gets her thrills from playing dress up and singing and dancing to Disney tunes. She's a whiner, too. But a cute whiner.

Like right now, as she hugged Eeyore and moaned about her wicked sister.

"C'mon, let's go downstairs." I yawned as I passed my desk, where my social studies folder caught my eye. Ugh. When was that monster due? I wished I could be one of those kids to whip out papers last minute, at the buzzer, without worrying. But I wasn't.

I grabbed the folder. "I'll be your bodyguard and you help me write my essay. Deal?"

"Deal," Gina said with a thumbs-up.

In the family room we stepped over Sophie, who was sprawled in front of the TV. I turned on the computer.

"What's your essay about?" Gina asked loudly over a commercial.

"Me, me, me, me," I sang like an opera star.

"I know where we can get pictures of you, Joseph."

"I don't need pictures. I need words, lots of them," I said, but Gina had already pulled down a mini-album from the bookcase and handed it to me.

She pointed to the label: TWINS' SECOND BIRTHDAY. "This one looks important."

I opened to a picture of my family in the backyard. Dad was holding Gina and I was holding Sophie. Mom was standing between us, dressed in spiky heels and squinting from the sun. Gina and Sophie wore matching polka-dot dresses and sparkly paper crowns.

I looked at my eight-year-old self. Stocky, with a crew cut and ears sticking out like coat hooks. And tan. It's silly how people call Asians yellow when my skin gets brick brown in summertime. Next to Dad, who's six-two and all muscle, I looked like a little puffer fish. I used to tell Dad that I wanted to grow up tall and strong like him. But he'd always answer the same way: "You're built like a fireplug, son. No one messes with fireplugs."

"How come you're not holding me?" Gina demanded, looking over my shoulder.

I shrugged. My sisters keep score of everything, from the number of squirts of chocolate syrup in their milk to how many times they get to sit by the car window.

Gina brought out a few more mini-albums. We looked

at everything from Mom and Dad's honeymoon photos to a picture of us three kids in the backseat of the van, holding Frazer after his hip surgery. Soon Sophie got bored with TV and hopped up beside us to look, too.

The more I stared at the pictures, the worse I felt about the essay. My parents have always acted like I was their firstborn—Italian just like them—and on most days it didn't bother me. But mirrors don't keep secrets and, like Mom's shop, our house is covered with mirrors. How many mornings had I jumped out of bed and stared into the dresser mirror, wondering who I looked like and who that person was? How many nights, while I brushed my teeth, had I studied my reflection, a face utterly unlike my sisters' or my parents'? Probably a million. And every time, I thought about that story of the emperor with no clothes. Was I the butt-naked emperor of Nutley, New Jersey, being duped into believing that I was Italian inside and out, because everyone was afraid to speak the truth?

I picked up my folder, pulled out the essay assignment, and reread it. Yikes! Dad always says the devil is in the details. The last line said the essay was due in nine days. Usually Mrs. Peroutka gives us over a month for writing assignments. How had I missed that?

Quickly I grabbed the phone. "Joseph here, desperate

to hire an Internet consultant."

"Sure," Nash answered. "Everything okay?"

"My essay is due sooner than I thought, all fifteen hundred words."

"I'm on it, Joseph. Anything special you want me to research about Korea?"

What did I want to find out, anyway? Enough to fill an autobiography. Or to help make my déjà-vu dream make sense. For years I'd had the same weird dream: me walking along a dirt road with other Koreans, but I didn't know who they were. I was pulling a red wagon, but I never knew where I was going. Everything was always fuzzy—especially faces.

But for now I had to stick with getting the essay finished. "Stuff about the city of Pusan. In Korea, back fourteen years ago when I was born, I guess. And if something comes up about a baby being found, that's even better."

"Do you know any details about where they found you or the time of day? The more specific, the better the chance I might uncover something."

"I know nothing," I replied, "but I'll try to ask my parents and get back to you."

• • •

"The old guy still has it!" Dad shouted as he sunk the ball into the hoop.

"The old guy got lucky," I snapped back.

Ouch. The basketball slapped my palm as I blocked Dad's next shot. Wrestling for the ball, he grabbed my waist and overpowered me. He used to box when he was young, and his arms are still thick and strong. I smacked his backside in a last-minute attempt to shake him, but he made the basket anyway.

The score was 5–2, and Dad was up. But I'm nothing if not persistent. A minute later, while Dad gushed in his greatness, I caught him off guard. I grabbed the ball, faked left, drove right, and made the layup.

"The hoop master scores!" I shouted, my fist raised to the sky.

"Not too bad for a young punk," Dad shouted just before he swiped the ball back and nailed the equivalent of an NBA three-pointer.

"Anytime, senior citizen!" I said, though I was the one breathing heavy.

We took a break. The sun shone directly overhead, and a warm breeze blew on the blacktop of Campbell Park Elementary School. My old stomping grounds, where Gina and Sophie were now in the second grade.

The air smelled of fresh-cut grass and tar from the resurfaced parking lot.

I guzzled from my water bottle. Our T-shirts lay balled up on the grass, soaked with sweat. A Little League game had started behind the school, and we heard cheering and clapping. Dad gazed toward the baseball fields. He gets quiet this time of year. Late spring is peak season for window washers. Mom says Dad is just exhausted from the long hours, but I don't think that's the only reason. I think he hates washing windows for a living, and it hits him more during the busy periods.

Mom told me that Dad didn't have the chance to go to college. The sons of Italian immigrants back then were expected to pick up a trade and start making money right after high school, like generations going back all the way to the old country. That's why New Jersey's yellow pages are still full of masons, plumbers, and carpenters with Italian names. Grandpa learned that new housing developments in northern Jersey needed window washers, so when Dad turned eighteen, his parents bought him a used pickup truck and painted "Calderaro Window Washers" on the side. That was the only career counseling he ever got.

"How's school going, Joseph?" Dad leaned back on the grass.

School made me think of my essay, but I decided to stick with good news first.

"I'm doing a drum solo for the concert next month," I said. At the Christmas show I'd played "Carol of the Bells" in a quartet. Dad practically climbed onstage to videotape me double-timing it between the timpani and the bells.

"A solo? Way to go. I bet your grandparents will come up from Florida for that. Joseph the Drummer Boy, that's what they call you."

"Just make sure Nonno Calderaro doesn't wear one of those loud orange shirts like he wore last year, okay?"

Dad laughed. "I'll try. So, how are grades?"

"I got an A plus on my science lab this week, and an eighty-four on my social studies quiz. It should've been a ninety, but Mrs. Peroutka gave tricky multiple-choice questions."

"No excuses, Joseph. You need top grades going into high school, and you're an honor student. Good job in science, though." He wiped his head with his T-shirt.

This was my first conversation with Dad lasting longer than thirty seconds since my birthday dinner. So far no one had drawn blood, so I figured I'd try him on the essay. Maybe he'd have an idea.

"Anything else you want to talk about?" he asked, as if he'd read my mind.

Call me Chicken Calderaro. Just thinking about this suddenly made me clammy. "I've got to write an essay, Dad, about my ancestry. Family roots from Korea, that sort of stuff." I bounced the basketball as I spoke. "But I don't know where to start."

Dad scratched his back. "I could tell you plenty of stories about Nonna and Nonno Calderaro. How they came from Siena, just south of Florence, in August of 1947."

I said nothing.

"New York City was an oven in the summertime back then," he continued. "Nonno told me it hit a hundred and three degrees when he and Nonna arrived, and the water fountain broke, no kidding. The only valuable thing Nonno brought from Italy was a pair of silver shears his father gave him. Which his father's father gave *him*.

"Both your grandparents worked in an upholstery factory in Brooklyn for three years, six days a week. They saved every nickel until they could open their own tailor shop." Dad paused, then added, "A tailor shop that made custom suits for Wall Street bankers."

I was listening, but honest to God, I didn't get Dad. He knew I'd heard Nonna and Nonno Calderaro's immigrant rags to middle-class riches story umpteen times. I knew things were hard back then. But why was *my* life hard for Dad to talk about? After all, he *chose* to adopt me.

Dad kept going on about the neighborhood his parents moved to after they opened the tailor shop. Italian Harlem, that's what they called it. I grew madder with each word. Why'd I ever think I could talk to him about this?

"They're not *my* ancestors," I blurted, interrupting Dad.

The Mad Meter suddenly switched on and started pulsing at an eighth-note tempo.

"That's a heck of a thing to say about your grandparents," he said.

"They're great, Dad. But I'm asking you about my *Korean* relatives, and you're not helping."

"I don't know any more than you do, Joseph. Talk to your mother about that."

Dad picked up his water bottle and T-shirt from the grass. Time to go home.

Talk to your mother, he'd said. As if I'd asked what's for dinner.

Towel Boy

On Monday afternoon the school bus screeched to a halt in front of the post office and I hopped off. Rain sprinkled on my face like salt on french fries. I was headed to the library. So far, the only thing Nash had found about the day I was born was that Pusan had set a record for rainfall. That would hardly take fifteen hundred words to describe. So I decided to get a few library books and load my essay up with a bunch of who-what-where facts about Korea—in case Nash didn't find anything in time. Maybe if my writing was clever enough, Mrs. Peroutka would forget about all that ancestry stuff.

First, though, I'd stop at Mom's shop to get money for a snack.

By the time I got to Shear Impressions, my backpack was soaked and my hair looked like black spaghetti. Nutley was setting its own record for rain.

"Joseph, my little water rat. Where's your umbrella?" Mom called from the register as she rang up a customer.

"Hold the flattery, Mom. I'm off to the library on an empty stomach. Can I have three bucks for a salad?"

"Salad my behind. You're headed to Randazzo's Bakery," she said.

Mom's customer handed her a tip and smiled as if she was in on the joke, too. She was one of what Mom calls her SOWS, Sweet Old Wash 'n' Setters.

Aunt Foxy walked out from the back room with her arms full of wet towels. She was dressed up fancy: a red satin blouse, huge hoop earrings, and a suede skirt, which meant she was over her recent wrecked romance. Aunt Foxy usually wears a sweat suit without makeup when she's recovering from a breakup. She's had plenty of boyfriends, but Mom says no one ever treats her good enough. Not that I'm betraying any deep family secrets by saying this stuff. You hang out in a hair salon for more than ten minutes and you could write a biography about any one of the hairdressers.

41

"I'm so happy to see my favorite teenaged godson," Aunt Foxy called out.

"Wouldn't have to do with that sack of towels, would it?" I pointed to the plastic bag she was filling on the floor.

She came over and gave me a hug. "Of course not."

I knew Aunt Foxy's joy had just as much to do with the towels as it did with my being her favorite godson. (I'm her only godson, by the way.) Whenever I walk into Shear Impressions, Mom and Aunt Foxy immediately see me as Joseph the Towel Boy. I've been carrying wet towels to Jiffy Wash Laundry ever since they bought the shop together five years ago.

Jiffy Wash was only a block away from the library, so I didn't mind running this errand. Besides, doing a good deed might earn me extra moolah to get *two* sprinkle cookies and a soda. *Niente per niente*. Mom taught me well.

Mom opened her purse. "Here's five dollars. Odd numbers are good luck," she said.

I stuck the money in my back pocket just as a tall, older girl walked in. She had a pierced nose and a butterfly tattoo on her shoulder. If I could've teleported a message to Mom and Aunt Foxy, it would have said, "Don't treat me like Towel Boy in front of *her*. Please."

42

But I wasn't so lucky.

Aunt Foxy rested the towel bag right smack in front of me. "I counted forty-six towels. This is heavy, so don't drag it on the sidewalk—it might rip."

The girl didn't even look at me. She grabbed a magazine and sat down. She probably thought I was a busboy from the Chinese restaurant across the street. People always think I'm Chinese; they think anyone with narrow eyes is. It used to bug me, but like Mom always says, you gotta get over the idiots in this world.

She was too old for me anyway. Besides, she wasn't as cute as Kelly.

Mrs. Faddegan flashed a toothy yellow smile as I dropped the towel bag on the counter.

"Thanks, Joseph. And tell your mom and Aunt Foxy that I'll stop over later to say good-bye."

"Good-bye?"

"Guess you didn't hear. We're moving to Florida. No more high taxes and damp winters for us."

Her news surprised me, though Mrs. Faddegan had been threatening to leave New Jersey for years.

"Herb and I bought a condo in Boca Raton," she said, sliding a brochure across the counter. "Comes with a community hot tub and free cable TV."

"Does that include HBO and Showtime?" I asked.

"I'm not sure," she answered, her face serious, like she wanted to call Florida to find out.

Mrs. Faddegan started to say something else, hesitated, and then started again. "You might like to know that the couple who bought the business are Korean." She spoke loud over the rumbling of washers and dryers.

I nodded, not sure what to say. Mostly I was wondering how I could get out of there fast. Everyone knew that Randazzo's ran out of sprinkle cookies around four o'clock, and I definitely didn't want their anisette cookies, which taste nasty, like black licorice.

"The new owners open tomorrow," she said. "They're from Flushing. Too crowded for them in the city, I guess. 'Course, I didn't tell them how traffic backs up on Grant Avenue once the packing plant lets out at five."

The Jiffy Wash was sticky hot, and the strong smell of bleach was giving me a headache. I had to hurry to get to Randazzo's and the library before they closed.

"Good-bye, Mrs. Faddegan. Good luck in Florida. And definitely get HBO. You deserve it."

Playing Bongos for the Gods

"Stop right there. Clarinets, start earlier—after the refrain," Mrs. Athena, our pint-sized band director, called from behind the podium. She lifted her mug toward the woodwind section in between sips of coffee.

We were warming up with "You're a Grand Old Flag." Mrs. Athena liked this tune a lot, I could tell. It's a peppy piece with cymbals crashing and trumpets blasting, but this morning it sounded sluggish, like funeral music.

"Where's that Uncle Sam spirit?" she asked. "Imagine it's the Fourth of July and you're marching down Main

Street, with thousands of patriotic folks cheering and waving little flags."

This time the clarinets came in a half note too late. And then all three bassoonists gave a not-me face when Mrs. Athena asked whose instrument was blowing like a moose with indigestion.

"I wish they'd get their woodwind act together," I whispered to Steve, who was slumped over the xylophone.

"No. No. No. The tempo is way off. Back to the first measure!" Mrs. Athena called, directing her words to the clarinets.

A collective groan came from the brass section and the percussion gang.

Steve tapped my head with the xylophone mallet. "I say we kidnap the woodwinds, tie them up with violin string, and hold them hostage in the custodian closet until school gets out."

"And make them listen to recordings of their own music," I added, grinning. People misjudge clarinet players as the true band kids because they're always walking around swinging their cases, but my ears have suffered the truth: most of them don't know a full note from a Post-it note.

We started over again. It still sounded bad. And again. Now it was badder than bad.

"Time out for an instrument check," Mrs. Athena announced, and she began walking from chair to chair, examining each clarinet like a laboratory specimen. I glanced over at the trumpets. Nash stared back and directed a thumbs-down at the clarinets.

"Here, Joseph," Jeff Henry whispered from the snare drum. "I saved some candy for you." He had a Three Musketeers bar tucked discreetly by his side, but Steve saw it too.

Steve tuned in when he heard "candy." "Got some for me?" he asked, almost drooling. Steve begs like a dog until he gets a piece of whatever you're eating. He actually looks like a Saint Bernard, with his square head and droopy eyes. A Saint Bernard with braces, that is.

I pulled my piece apart and handed half to him on the sly. Mrs. Athena was still looking at clarinets, and I didn't want to get caught breaking the No Food rule. I glanced over at the flutes.

"Pssst. Joseph."

Robyn was whispering loudly from the flute section. She put her flute between her knees, grabbed her eyelids with her fingertips, and popped them inside out so she looked like Tweetie Bird. Her lashes were sticking straight up, and I could see the whites of her eyeballs.

Nothing unusual. Robyn and I always do juvenile

stuff to shock each other.

She was waiting for my comeback, so I stuck my drumsticks in my ears and started rocking back and forth while I crossed my eyes and stuck out my tongue. Robyn giggled, then covered her mouth to prevent a full-blown laugh attack.

"Aha, as I suspected, a cracked reed," Mrs. Athena said to a sixth grader. She helped replace it, and we picked up where we left off. Surprise, surprise, we sounded cheery. And patriotic. And in sync. I could see the flags waving now.

"Finally!" Mrs. Athena called, jumping pogo stick–style. "Let's celebrate with a trip to the Caribbean."

"Jamaican Farewell," my favorite. Just tapping to that calypso beat works like a natural antidepressant for me. This sounds crazy, but it's true: I was born in Korea and my family is Italian, but I've got the soul of a reggae drummer.

Nash once told me I get this faraway look in my eyes when we play "Jamaican Farewell." He said my shoulders move up and down to the beat, like I'm sitting on top of a mountain playing bongos for the gods.

He's right. When my drumsticks are tapping, I'm gone to Planet Harmony. Nothing else matters. Not Kelly, not my essay, nothing. It felt that way from the first time

I played rudiments in fourth grade. Drumming must be in my blood. Maybe my birth father is a drummer in Pusan.

"Hey, Joseph, check out the new kid," Steve said. He pointed a mallet toward the flute section.

Talk about being distracted. I hadn't even noticed the unfamiliar face only a few seats down from Robyn.

The new kid had thick black glasses. He was squinting as he read his music, and he was wearing a pink sport shirt. Pink, with a collar, on a regular school day. I kept looking over at him in between full measure rests.

He was Korean. I just knew it. There was something about how his bangs spiked up like teeny black porcupine quills. Like mine.

Round and round my sisters spun.

"They don't give refunds if you puke," I whispered that afternoon to Sophie and Gina, who were squeezed next to each other in the same stylist chair. Their knees were pulled up to their chests, lollipops were sticking out of their mouths, and they were grinning like they were on a roller coaster.

As soon as Mom walked over, Sophie stuck her foot down and stopped moving.

"Hi, honey. Didn't see you come in. Are you busy?" Mom asked me.

Translation: Time for a walk, Towel Boy.

Before I could answer, she handed me a bag of dirty towels and some money. "Here, get yourself something at Randazzo's on the way. But don't forget the towels. There's thirty-five in there."

"I need some amaretti, Mommy. They're my favorite cookies. Can I go with Joseph?" Sophie asked.

"Me too. *Pleeease?*" Gina added.

"You both had a snack already. Study for your spelling quiz." Mom pointed at their backpacks and covered her ears as the twins wailed.

"Want some biscotti?" I called to Aunt Foxy at her station.

"I'd love some, but I better pass. Gotta get more fiber in my diet."

Nothing is private in a hair salon: constipation, cheating boyfriends, bad grades. Nothing.

After Randazzo's, I headed toward the Jiffy Wash Laundry. I was expecting the usual thirty-second chitchat with Mrs. Faddegan. I'd forgotten that she'd sold the business until I pulled open the door and nearly plowed into the new kid from band.

"Hey!" I said, surprised and a little embarrassed.

"Hey back," he said with a laugh. He was holding a soda and a deck of cards.

He was at least two inches shorter than me and had a narrow face. But we both had the same nose: wide and smooth with a flat bridge. Koreans are a bridgeless bunch, which causes problems when you try to impress a girl. One minute you're talking, and the next you look down and your sunglasses fall off.

"I'm Joseph," I said. "Joseph Calderaro. I saw you in band. I play drums."

"I'm Yongsu Han. Mrs. Athena told me about you."

"Don't believe everything she says. She just wants to keep me from joining chorus."

He laughed. "Today was my first day. I'm in eighth grade. You?"

"Today was my hundred and fifty-ninth day of school, and you can bet I'm still counting," I replied. "I'm in eighth grade too."

I dropped the sack of towels on the counter, noticing the bag had a slight rip in the bottom.

"*Uhmma!*" he called into the back room. Or something like that. No *Uhmma* came, though the mail carrier walked in and handed the new kid a stack of letters.

"You're Korean, too?" Yongsu asked.

"Sort of," I said.

He pushed his glasses back on his nose. The way a geek would right before the bully pops him.

A woman walked out from the back room. Korean, of course, so I figured *Uhmma* meant "Mom." Suddenly I felt out of place. Like how a Vulcan would feel at a Romulan festival in an old *Star Trek* episode. The Hans were *real* Koreans.

The new kid's mom held an armful of tangled wire hangers, which she threw in a plastic bin beside the cash register.

Then she spun around and noticed me. She lifted her eyebrows slightly, like she was suspicious, and grinned, showing big teeth. Not exactly buckteeth, like Mom says mine would be if she and Dad hadn't dropped three grand on my braces, but big like horse teeth, with a lot of gum.

"Ahn nyong ha seh yo?" she said.

Both Yongsu and his mother stared at me.

I shrugged. "I don't know any Korean."

The new kid said something in Korean, and his mom nodded. She started pulling wet towels out of the sack and counting them.

"There's thirty-five," I said, remembering what Mom said.

But she counted anyway. So much for trust among Koreans.

"What's your family name?" Her accent sounded

52

much thicker than Yongsu's.

"Calderaro," I said, speaking slowly. Up went her suspicious eyebrows. "The towels are from my mom's shop. She's a hairdresser."

"You're missing one towel."

I felt like she was accusing me.

"Maybe it fell." I pointed to the floor on her side of the counter. She bent over and picked up a towel.

"Your mom Korean?" she asked as she reached for an order slip. Her eyes sparkled as she spoke, a little like Gina's when she's got a secret.

"No, she's Italian. My dad, too. But I'm Korean, which you probably figured out," I said as my mouth started running away from my face.

Mrs. Han didn't understand.

"I'm adopted," I explained.

Mrs. Han stared at me with icy eyes, but didn't say a word. It was as if she'd taken out a name tag, scribbled "fake Korean" on it, and stuck it to my T-shirt.

Then she muttered something quickly in Korean to her son. He picked up the towels and carried them to the back room. A bell jingled as another customer walked in.

"Phone number?" Mrs. Han asked, and I rattled off the number for Shear Impressions. She tore the yellow customer's copy from the order slip and handed it to me.

Mrs. Faddegan never used slips. She just billed Mom and Aunt Foxy once a month.

Mrs. Han quickly turned her attention to a man who'd just dropped a bunch of shirts on the counter.

No good-bye, no thank you from Uhmma.

I pushed hard on the door to get the heck outta there.

"Joseph, wait!"

"Whaddaya want?" I snapped with as much Jersey attitude as I could muster. The Hans could go back to doing laundry in Flushing, if that was even what they did there. Or better yet, Korea.

"You like to play war or poker?" The new kid was still holding the deck of cards.

The thought of playing cards in this sticky place was about as appealing as the stomach flu on Christmas morning.

"It's too hot in here." I kept on walking.

He followed me outside. "We'll play behind the store. You like soda? We've got cans in the fridge, in the back room. Ginger ale, orange, root beer, whatever you like."

I was about to say no again. Why should I spend time with this guy? But then again, my other options weren't so great: either walking the two miles home to get going on my social studies essay or hanging around Shear

Impressions for a couple of hours and listening to the hairdressers' gossip, since I knew Mom had back-to-back appointments until seven.

And root beer *was* my favorite.

"Okay," I said. "What's your name again?"

He smiled. "Yongsu Han."

The back of the building had two tiny windows that reminded me of portholes on a submarine. One was blocked by an air conditioner. The other had a ripped screen. Yongsu and I started playing war on the rusted metal picnic table, on a patch of brown grass beside the parking lot. I took a long swig of root beer. I'd never heard of this brand, but it sure was cold and bubbly.

I looked up and saw Mrs. Han staring from one of the windows. I could tell she was scowling. She wasn't discreet, the way Mom is when she peeks through the dining room curtain at our neighbor whose boyfriend drives a Harley and wears leather everything.

Obviously Mrs. Han thought I was a cheap Korean imitation, maybe even a troublemaker who needed watching. It hurt my ego, because most of my friends' parents make a big fuss over me, like I'm this funny, well-balanced influence on their kids. I thought about asking

55

Yongsu what was up with his mom, but he seemed so thrilled to have me around that I couldn't do it.

"Let's switch to blackjack," I said. "I'll deal."

I shuffled the deck while he got up and threw his soda can in the Dumpster. A breeze blew, and I smelled hamburgers from the diner across the street. My stomach growled.

"Hit me," Yongsu said after I dealt his top card. I gave him another card. He had a ten of diamonds on top of a nine of clubs showing.

"I'm over." He flipped his bottom card. Six of spades. The wind stirred and sent the card flying off the table. He bent down to grab it just as a white hatchback pulled up.

Yongsu ran over, and a Korean man got out of the car. Yongsu bowed, and the man nodded back. Must be his dad, I figured. They talked, and the man looked over and waved to me.

Clearly Yongsu inherited his friendly gene from his paternal side.

They walked to the rear entrance. Then Yongsu ran back and began shuffling the cards.

"Was that your *Uhppa*?" I said, remembering how he'd called his mom *Uhmma*.

"*Apa*," he corrected. "You say '*Apoji*' when you're older."

"So you speak perfect Korean?"

"I lived in Korea till I was seven. You know any Koreans here?"

"Not really." Of course, I always notice other Asian kids. But in my school, if they're not in your classes, your neighborhood, or your after-school activities, they might as well live in Antarctica.

The wind picked up again suddenly, and I wished I'd worn my band jacket.

Yongsu told me he had a sister who was also in eighth grade. She hadn't moved yet because she was in a gifted music program. She'd already composed a piano piece that her school orchestra performed at a state competition.

"You're twins?" I asked.

He dealt the cards. "No, she skipped a year back in grade school."

"I've got twin sisters," I told Yongsu.

"You're a triplet?" he asked, confused.

I explained that my sisters were younger and not adopted.

"My sister's staying with my aunt and uncle in Flushing for a few more days until the music program is over," he said.

"What's her name?"

"Ok-hee."

I must have made a face.

"Ok-hee's a popular name in Korea," he said. "Like Brittney or Jessica in America."

"Or Kelly." Popular with me, for sure.

We stopped playing cards. Yongsu took a handheld computer out of his pocket. It was a Japanese video game he'd bought off a street vendor in Flushing. It played like a space arcade, but involved morphed grasshoppers searching for food and fighting four-legged bad guys.

"You ever heard the name Duk-kee before?" I asked.

"One of my best friends in Taegu was Duk-kee."

He pronounced "Duk-kee" differently. More like "Took-ee." Not "Ducky," the way I say it.

"Do you know where you were born in Korea, Joseph?"

"Pusan," I said. "You been there?"

He nodded. "It's a two-hour drive from Taegu, where we lived. In the summer my parents took us to the fish market and beach in Pusan. My cousin goes to university there."

I wished I had a Korean cousin. Then I could write about him or her for my essay. I'd settle for just about any Korean relative at this point.

"Yongsu, can you think of any famous Koreans? Like how we have George Washington and Tiger Woods?"

His eyes sparkled like his mom's. "You ask funny questions."

"I'm not kidding," I said. "It's for a school paper."

Yongsu said there were plenty. His dad had shelves of Korean history books.

"Problem is they're written in Korean," he said.

"Yeah, that's a big problem for me." I glanced at my watch. It was five thirty. I was starving, and that burger smell was torturing me.

"Yongsu!" his mom called from the window. She shouted something in Korean, and even I could figure out it meant "Get your butt inside."

On my way back to Shear Impressions, I practiced saying my Korean name, Duk-kee, the way Yongsu had pronounced it. But it just didn't sound right coming out of my mouth.

Sounds like Baby Moses

Mom came home from work as the sun was setting on Wednesday. She had dark circles under her eyes and a cardboard box of fried chicken in her hands.

"I had one heck of an afternoon perming crabby Mrs. Congelosi. After an hour of wrapping her whole head in medium-sized silver rollers—and listening to her complain about her daughter-in-law—she changes her mind and says she wants tight *blue* rollers. And then she had the nerve to tell *me* to hurry up! No way am I cooking," she declared.

Dad took the chicken from Mom and wrapped his arms around her. "Aristotle said beauty is a gift from God. Let me behold the present He's bestowed on me!"

"Oh, spare me your Greek philosophy and kiss me," she said.

They kissed, this drawn-out smooch that made me feel embarrassed. Mom and Dad may be over forty and set in their suburban ways, but they still act like they've got raging hormones.

Luckily my sisters didn't see them lock lips. That always gets them squealing and making "yuck faces." They were in the family room, working on a thousand-piece Noah's Ark puzzle—which, of course, would never get assembled without a fight and pathetic pleas for help.

Dad opened the back sliding door. "I'm going to water the tomato plants."

"I'll set the table," I said.

"That would be nice, Joseph," Mom said, looking surprised. I don't usually jump up at the chance to help in the kitchen.

Alone at last with Mom. I could ask what she knew about the day I was born. Seeing Yongsu and his parents got me wondering even more. Plus, I still had to give Nash some more info for the search, since my talk with Dad was a bust.

"Can I ask you a few questions, Mom?"

She gave me a curious look. "Ask away."

"Do you know my birth parents' names, or where the adoption agency found me?" I folded the napkins in triangles, concentrating so I wouldn't have to look at her.

Mom started to say something, then paused. "I planned on sharing this with you at a special time. When you were . . . well, a bit older."

"Sharing what?" I asked.

"The information the adoption agency gave us. But it isn't much, Joseph."

"I really want to know whatever it is," I pleaded. "Now."

She took a breath before she began. "They told us they found you in the south of Pusan, by the waterfront, in a police station parking lot. An old woman was walking back from the fish market in the afternoon when she heard a baby crying. You were lying in a basket, wrapped in a blanket."

This sounded like the Baby Moses story. Had I floated down a river in Pusan too?

"What was my birth mother's name?"

"They didn't give us any names."

"What day did the old woman find me?"

"May seventh," Mom said, rubbing the top of my head with her fingertips.

"Well, since my birthday is May fifth, that meant my birth mother took care of me for two days. Maybe she felt torn and didn't want to give me up," I said.

Mom nodded. I noticed her eyes were watery. It made me feel kind of guilty.

"Move, Frazer!" Sophie yelled from the family room. That old boxer loved to park himself in inconvenient places, like right on top of the puzzle.

"What's got you thinking about all this, honey?" Mom asked.

Should I tell her about the essay? I wanted to, but she was practically crying already. I didn't want to make her feel like she wasn't a good-enough mom.

"I just met this new kid at school today, and he's Korean. That's all."

She nodded and started scooping mashed potatoes from the plastic container onto the plates. She didn't seem as upset anymore.

I kept imagining how it all happened in Pusan fourteen years ago. "Maybe it was a baby-snatching conspiracy and the lady who found me was in on it," I said. "She could have kidnapped me, realized she was going to get caught, and then dropped me at the police station with that story so they wouldn't suspect anything."

"I don't think so," Mom answered. "The adoption

agency told us that's just the way babies are left in Korea. Birth mothers pick spots where they know their babies will be safe and get discovered quickly."

Then Mom continued, as if trying to convince me she was right. "Unmarried Korean women can't keep their babies, Joseph. Having a child before marriage is taboo there, much worse than here. Mothers without husbands are outcasts. Sometimes they can't even find jobs or homes. I think your birth mother knew you both would have had a difficult life if she'd kept you."

"Why do Koreans make the mothers feel so bad?" I asked. "That's dumb."

"I've read that Koreans have mixed feelings about adoption. Some think it's unnatural, but others feel terrible that they don't do a better job taking care of children in their country. I think it's so sad, especially for the birth mothers."

I thought about Mrs. Han's face when I said I was adopted. I must have been a breathing reminder of all those abandoned babies back in her country. "Well, maybe my birth mother *was* married to my birth father and they just didn't have enough money to raise a kid," I said. "Or she could have gotten sick. Isn't that possible too?"

"I suppose," Mom said, nodding, although she looked doubtful.

Through the window I watched Dad reel the hose in. I better wrap this up.

"Do you know anything else? I mean, about me before America?"

Mom closed her eyes as if she were thinking hard.

"Your birth mother had tucked a note under your blanket. We never got it—and I'm sure it was written in Korean—but the adoption agency told us about it. She asked that you be raised Christian. That's part of the reason you came to us."

"What about my Korean name, Duk-kee?" I asked, just as Dad opened the sliding glass door.

"Just what I've told you already, honey. Your birth mother named you Duk-kee. It's a common name in Korea."

Dad came inside and washed his hands. "What are you two talking about?"

"Joseph was asking about the day he was born and his name. His Korean name," she said.

Dad nodded and looked at me. "Your mom was set on naming you Joseph after the saint when you arrived safely, but I was partial to Antonio."

"Yeah, Dad, I sure look like an Antonio." I was teasing, but I wasn't, too.

"We could've picked worse. You could've been

baptized . . . Luigi!" He shouted it loud, intentionally exaggerating an Italian accent.

"Luigi?" I made my ultra-disgusted face.

"Don't pay any attention to your father. He wanted Gina to be named Philomena. I put my foot down on that one." She was unscrewing the cork from a bottle of merlot, Dad's favorite.

"Thanks for talking, Mom," I said. I felt bad inside. Like I should have said, "None of this matters. You're my real mom, after all."

"Anytime you wanna talk, Joseph, we talk."

I couldn't talk anymore, even if I wanted to. My head hurt from all this heavy info. I would call Nash and tell him everything after dinner, but for now I didn't want to think about it.

"Gina, you're messing up the whole puzzle!" Sophie shouted. "The camel's hump doesn't go behind the zebra's tail."

"Don't blame me. Noah brought too many animals on this ark," Gina whined. "Can you help us, Joseph?"

I sat on the carpet next to my sisters and picked up a puzzle piece—an orange striped tail. "Let's get this ark built so these fur balls don't drown. Besides, chow's on the table and my stomach is growling like this tiger."

Starstruck

"Go away," I shouted, knowing the Lilliputian knocking on the other side of the door was one of my sisters.

Who *wouldn't* be grouchy? I was trapped in my bedroom dungeon, slaving away on my essay. My doomed essay. Even with all the details I had given him, Nash still couldn't find anything. *And* his computer crashed. He said it had some sort of virus—probably caused by the *malocchio* since I wasn't wearing my goat horn.

It was still sunny out, and the sound of kids playing in the distance was dogging me.

I picked up one of the library books. It had a map of North and South Korea on the cover and a photo of Mount Hallasan, the tallest mountain in South Korea.

I reread the assignment sheet for the twentieth time: "Your essay must fully explore your ancestry and reflect on its impact on your life."

Why did Mrs. Peroutka have to turn social studies into soul searching?

"Guess what, Joseph!" Gina squeaked from the hallway.

"What?"

"We're making chocolate chip milkshakes!"

"Bring one up to me. I'm busy."

I heard Gina run downstairs and then back upstairs again. "Mommy says no food out of the kitchen. You know the rule. Come down," she pleaded again.

"Maybe later."

After scanning a hundred pages in the book, my yellow notepad was still wordless. The "I've Got Nothing to Say Korean Heritage Tale" by Joseph Calderaro.

Dozens and dozens of Korean faces stared up at me from the pages. People from the Yi Dynasty all the way to the Korean War, and yet I couldn't find a way to get started. To stick *me* in the story.

A couple of pictures showed Koreans who led this

68

surprise counterattack when Japan invaded in 1910. I never knew that Japan invaded Korea. Or that these scrappy Korean nationalists waged such a fight against the odds to resist. They reminded me of minutemen from the Revolutionary War, except with black hair, buttonhole eyes, and swords instead of rifles.

A few pages later I saw this faded photo of a short, muscular Korean runner. He wore a medal around his neck and he looked serious, like most people in old pictures. Yet there was something bold about him, with his defiant eyes, spiky hair, and puckered lips, ready to take on the world. He had something to prove.

The photo caption said his name was Sohn Kee Chung. He won a gold medal for the men's marathon at the 1936 Olympics in Berlin. They called it "Hitler's Games" because it was right before World War II, when Hitler used the Olympics to show off his power.

Sohn Kee Chung represented Japan, which occupied Korea. He probably looked mad because he had to wear a Japanese team jersey, the trademark of the invaders.

Now *here* was a Korean who inspired me. Someone I could relate to . . . and *be* related to? Maybe Sohn Kee Chung could be my grandfather, and I could write my essay about *him*! Why not? It was a harmless idea. Mrs. Peroutka would get all gaga when she read my saga, I'd get a good grade, and my parents and I would avoid any more painful pangs caused by talking about adoption.

"Last chance for a milkshake, Joseph," Gina called from downstairs. "And just for you, we used *real* chocolate bars and Lactaid milk to make them!"

Real chocolate bars? "Okay, okay, I'm coming!" I saved my place in the book. Now the essay actually seemed doable. Still a pain in the butt, but at least I had a cool name and face to relate to.

"Not too short around the ears," I told Aunt Foxy as she snipped away at my hair.

"Don't worry," she said. She knew I didn't want my ears sticking out like a Chihuahua's.

Aunt Foxy has cut my hair ever since I started middle school. That's because Mom can't resist the temptation to style my hair like an upside-down bowl, the way she did in my preschool days. So Mom and I struck a deal. Aunt Foxy is allowed to cut my hair any way I want and Mom can't say boo—as long as I don't pierce any body parts.

Aunt Foxy was snipping along my neck and talking with Mom, who was at the sink rinsing Mrs. Bertolotti's body wave.

"What a jerk Walt turned out to be," Aunt Foxy said.

"Cheap, too. He actually expected *me* to pay for the cheesecake and espresso last night. This, after he told me we were through!"

"Good riddance to him. What's that saying? A woman without a man is like a fish without a bicycle," Mom said.

"Without *two* bicycles," Aunt Foxy added, laughing. Then she looked down and smiled. "A friend of yours came in for a cut and blow-dry the other day, Joseph."

"Who?"

"A blonde with natural highlights. Hair past her shoulders and no split ends."

"She have a name?"

"Kelly, I think it was."

Wow! Just days ago, Kelly Gerken had sat in this very chair. I felt starstruck, like when you go to a restaurant and see a framed photo of a celebrity dining there.

"She said we were *friends*?"

"She said a lot more than that—how funny you are and how you make her laugh. She's a looker all right, and very picky about her hair. If she weren't your friend, I would've told her to chill out, what with all her bossy orders about evening out her layers."

She thinks I'm funny? I make her laugh?

Mrs. Bertolotti shuffled back from the sink to Mom's cutting station. The lady walked so slow it shouldn't even be called walking, but she'd had a stroke a few years ago and was way up there in years.

"Since when does Kelly come here for haircuts?" I asked.

"Since Tiffany, that wenchy hairdresser at Beau Coup, ran off to LA and deserted her customers." Aunt Foxy ran the razor across what I call my sideburns.

"Did Kelly say anything about having a boyfriend?"

"Nope. Besides, Joseph, it doesn't matter. At your age boyfriends are like credit cards. A girl can switch any time she gets a better deal."

Aunt Foxy sprinkled talc on my neck and unfastened the plastic smock. I got up and saw Mrs. Bertolotti was still only halfway to Mom's station. I took her arm and helped her along. She smiled through thick glasses that made her blue eyes look like giant gum balls.

"You're going to make one fine husband, Joseph," she said. Her bony hand trembled, and she smelled like roses.

"I hope Mr. Bertolotti doesn't catch us arm in arm like this," I said, and she chuckled.

I smiled back. I liked making Mrs. Bertolotti laugh. And I'd finally gotten my foot in the door of Kelly's world.

Courting Miss MVP

The curse of a superstitious Italian mother struck again. No wonder I felt nervous that Friday the thirteenth was C-day, as Frankie calls it when you make contact with a girl for the first time.

That afternoon was Kelly's softball game, and I was asking her to the movies afterward. No matter what. Aunt Foxy's words echoed in my mind: "You make her laugh." If only I could get Kelly to share popcorn and a box of Junior Mints, who knows? Maybe going to the Farewell Formal together wasn't the impossible dream.

"It's about time you showed up, Joseph!" Frankie

called from the top row of bleachers. A pair of binoculars hung around his neck, and he kept looking through them every few seconds.

I climbed the bleachers reluctantly and sat next to Frankie. He can be really annoying sometimes.

Frankie stood up and pointed the binoculars at our team's dugout. "Yes, folks, the Frankie radar is scanning the playing field. Numbers one and two are in the dugout, and number three is up at bat."

"What are you talking about?" I squinted as I looked at the players. The batter's jersey number was twelve, not three.

"Sherrie Harrington, Tara Riddle, and Molly Palanski. They don't know it, but they're all finalists in my Farewell Formal date selection."

I groaned. "What inning is this?"

"Bottom of the third. We're up 3–1. Kelly's pitching great. They only got one hit off her in the last inning."

I looked over to the dugout. An assistant coach was explaining something to Kelly, but she looked like she didn't want to hear it.

I wiped my forehead, pulled my water bottle from my backpack, and took a gulp. On the lower bleachers I noticed Yongsu, wearing another collared shirt—a white one this time. Like a kid in private school.

He must have sensed someone was staring at him because he looked up and began waving like crazy, as if I couldn't see him from ten feet away. Then he grabbed his flute case and books and climbed up the bleachers to join us.

"Who's this nerd?" Frankie whispered as Yongsu approached.

"Yongsu Han. He's new. And anybody who eats fluffernutter sandwiches in middle school shouldn't be calling anyone else a nerd."

That zipped Frankie's lips temporarily.

Yongsu sat next to me. He had a bag of Cheetos under his arm. "So you're a softball fan?" I asked.

"My sister, Ok-hee, joined the team." He pointed toward the bench.

"I thought she was in Flushing. At some fancy music program."

"She finished. The coach said she was good enough to make the team, but she has to practice before playing in a game," he said, in between mouthfuls.

This my-sister-is-a-superstar talk was almost too much. "Piano, school, softball . . . is there *anywhere* your sister doesn't kick butt?"

"Cleaning her room." He grinned. "She's a slob."

I looked down at our team. Ok-hee sat on the bench

next to the coach. She had super-long hair. Long legs, too. I could tell she was taller than Yongsu, even though she was younger.

"What are you doing here?" Yongsu asked me.

Frankie blurted out my answer. "Joseph's trying to pitch himself to the pitcher."

The other team was up at bat now. It was the top of the fourth and Kelly just threw a beauty, a perfect strike. Cheers roared from our section of the bleachers. None louder than mine.

Yongsu's eyes scanned the softball field. I had this hunch that, in Frankie's terms, he was a zero-contact kind of guy. He hadn't discovered the agony and the ecstasy of girls yet.

"Did you find a famous Korean for your paper?" Yongsu asked.

"Yeah. Now I have to write about him," I said.

"Who'd you pick?"

"Sohn Kee Chung, the Olympic marathoner." I skipped over how I planned to magically make him my grandfather.

Yongsu nodded. "My father's told me stories about him. He was fast! And brave, too, even when Japan was bullying Korea. Good choice, Joseph."

"Thanks," I said. But I wondered if I *was* making a

good choice. Sohn Kee Chung was brave for sure, but was I? Maybe I was taking the easy way out. I didn't want to cheat, and I knew this Korean gold medalist would never have cheated.

But then again, Sohn Kee Chung didn't have an ancestry essay to turn in to Mrs. Peroutka, either.

Frankie left for the late bus at the top of the sixth, just after the other team scored. But then our team caught a hitting fever. Janice Reed slammed a double, and then Kelly hit a line drive for a single, bringing Janice to third. I started whooping and hollering and even shouted out some rhyming raps. I thought I saw Ok-hee glare at me. Maybe I'd interrupted her Zen concentration on the game. Or maybe she was just looking for her brother.

Just as I shoved a handful of Cheetos in my mouth, Yongsu tapped my shoulder.

"About my mom," he said, "she doesn't understand adoption. She says it's not natural for parents to raise other people's kids. Sorry if she hurt your feelings."

He was staring down at the ground under the bleachers. I could tell he felt embarrassed.

"Let's forget it," I said, reaching for more Cheetos. What did I care about Mrs. Han? There were plenty of Americans, including my own family, who didn't understand adoption either.

Our team won 7–2. Kelly brought in two runs in the top of the seventh with a triple to right field. I stood outside the exit of the locker room afterward, ready to ask her out. Yongsu hovered nearby, waiting for his sister. He was doing yo-yo tricks like Walk the Dog and Around the World, and even got the yo-yo to land in his palm.

Kelly's parents were talking to Coach Durrey. Mrs. Gerken had diamond earrings as big as peanut M&M's, and the shine on Mr. Gerken's shoes was visible from ten feet away. And even I could tell the peach fuzz on his head was probably from an anti-balding drug.

Dad's bald spot is double the size of Mr. Gerken's, but the only thing he puts on it is sunscreen.

Watching them, I wondered what they'd think about me if I walked into their mansion with Kelly. Maybe they'd recognize the name Calderaro and realize I was a window washer's son.

Nah, they wouldn't get the Calderaro connection. I bet they'd never talked to a kid who looked like me before, except maybe someone washing dishes in one of their restaurants.

I was starting to get antsy when Robyn and a couple of other band kids appeared, swinging their instrument cases. They shouted for me to come over—they were tossing a water balloon around—but I said I couldn't. I had business to attend to. Then Yongsu's sister came out, her arms full of books. Yongsu ran toward her.

"Ok-hee, this is Joseph, my friend I've been talking about," he said.

She nodded and looked me up and down. Like mother, like daughter. Nothing about Ok-hee suggested she'd been Flushing's Miss Congeniality.

"Is Coach Durrey going to let you play in the next game?" I asked.

"I need a full week of practices," she answered coolly.

"Good luck." I gestured like I was swinging a bat. "New Jersey pitchers try to get you to swing at wild balls, but you just need to hold your ground."

She looked at me like I was a moron. What, did you have to be a major-league coach before you could offer advice?

Ok-hee dropped a book as she walked away. I picked it up and recognized the title: *A Spell for Chameleon*.

"That's the best of the Xanth series," I said. "Did you get to the part where Bink meets up with Evil Magician Trent?"

She gave me a doubting glare like she didn't expect anyone with below a Mensa IQ to read anything but easy readers. Yongsu shrugged like he was used to his sister's moods and waved good-bye cheerfully.

Watching Yongsu and Ok-hee walk away got me wondering again. Maybe I had a snooty know-it-all sister in Korea who was a foot taller than me. Maybe I had a couple of brothers and sisters. Now I wanted to know if I did. I *really* wanted to know. And not just for a social studies essay, either.

Another five minutes passed and I almost left too, because I figured Dad was waiting to pick me up and getting grouchy. But finally Kelly came out of the locker room. She'd pitched five tough innings and still looked like a model. Wow.

I intercepted her before she reached her parents. "Awesome triple, Miss MVP!" I called.

"Thanks, Joseph." She flashed a grin.

Her smile sent me soaring. Go for it, Joseph. I pumped myself up. "I was wondering if you wanted to go to the movies tomorrow," I began. I couldn't stop now. "Maybe we can get some pizza afterward. At Dom's across from the CinemaPlex. We could walk there."

She didn't look horrified. A good sign.

"Dom's has free soda refills and the best Sicilian pizza in New Jersey," I added.

"I like regular pizza."

"Their regular pizza is twice as good as their Sicilian. Trust me, my record is five pieces."

She laughed. Then Mr. Gerken called her. He sounded like he was in a hurry.

"I've got a softball lesson tomorrow. How about Sunday?" she asked.

"Lucky for you I've had a cancellation. I'm available on Sunday, say twelve thirty?" I had no idea what movie would be playing, but it didn't matter. Even a Disney cartoon would do.

"Sounds good. I'll meet you at the CinemaPlex then," she said as she flung her hot pink gym bag over her shoulder and walked off.

I waited until the Gerkens' car drove off before letting loose with "Woo-hoo, I'm the *man*!" Then I danced a touchdown dance in the parking lot, just as Dad's truck pulled up.

Run, Grandpa, Run

eck, peck, peck, peck.

My fingers hacked away at the keyboard Saturday night. I clicked the mouse to check the word count: 1295. Roughly two hundred words away from the essay finish line. And just in time, too. It was due Monday, but tomorrow was my movie date with Kelly.

The freezer door slammed shut. From the computer desk in the family room, I watched my sisters battle by the kitchen counter. Their hair was wet and braided and they were already in their pajamas. Mom was working at the beauty shop later than usual, leading new product training for the hairdressers. Dad was in his recliner, reading another classic that you'd expect to find in the hands of a pipe-smoking professor, not a window washer who looks tough in a tank top.

"Give that to me!" Gina yelled. "Daddy, Sophie took the last Popsicle!"

Sophie sat on a kitchen stool gripping the Popsicle like a weapon. "I grabbed it first. Fair and square."

The air was thick as oatmeal. No matter how many times I wiped my forehead, it felt greasy. My glass of fruit punch sat in a puddle next to the mouse pad.

"Bully!" Gina wailed.

"Both of you have cookies if there aren't enough Popsicles," Dad growled from behind *The Brothers Karamazov*.

"I don't want cookies," Gina whined.

"I'm eating this Popsicle. I got it first." Sophie ripped the wrapper off just as Gina started crying.

"Maybe there are more in the back of the freezer." Dad put his book down and walked into the kitchen.

I hit my mental button to mute the sibling static. I was on a roll, two-finger punching at the keyboard.

The title of my essay was "A Medal for Speed and a Life of Honor: My Grandpa Sohn." I wrote how Sohn Kee Chung was my father's father. Since I couldn't find where he was born, I picked Yongsu's birthplace, Taegu. Dad's atlas listed Taegu as the third-largest city in South Korea, right along the Naktong River. It was a city that used to be famous for apples—"Best in Asia," according to the atlas—so I gave Grandpa Sohn's family their very own orchard.

A young man can only pick apples for so long. Out of sheer boredom, young Sohn began challenging his six sisters and brothers to footraces in the orchard.

Racing became a nightly ritual, I wrote, after the day's picking was done. Sohn's father always served as judge at the finish line, though none of his siblings could catch up with Sohn. Afterward the Chung family would sit down together to eat rice and kimchi, a spicy pickled cabbage. It sounded like Koreans eat kimchi the way Italians eat pasta. All the time.

When Sohn was older, people started noticing how fast he could run. His father realized that Sohn had talent and encouraged him to train, which was pretty decent considering that meant one less set of hands picking all those apples.

As I unwound this story, I felt like I'd gotten into the real Sohn's head. Like I understood how outraged he must have felt about the Japanese taking over his country. How lousy it must have been to represent Japan, the invader, in track and field—*his* sport. The Japanese government looked down on the Koreans like the Nazis did the Jews, wanting to kill off everything Korean. Clothes. Tradition. Even their Korean names.

Sohn didn't want to wear Japan's colors on the Olympic team. But what choice did he have? He could either run representing Japan, or stay home, give up his dream, and pick apples forever.

I wrote that Grandpa Sohn stuffed his sneakers and a pair of chopsticks in his gym bag. Then, with the rally cry, "This one's for Korea," he headed to the 1936 Berlin games. It was the first time he'd ever left Taegu. But he never forgot he was Korean. Even during the Olympics, when the Japanese forced him to use the name Kitei Son, he protested in his own way—by sketching a tiny map of Korea next to his signature.

The library book described Sohn's butt-kicking victory over the other marathoners in Berlin, including a heavily favored Argentinian named Juan Zabala. Adolf

Hitler, who people called the führer, was rooting for Zabala—probably because Zabala looked more like him than Sohn did. But Hitler didn't know he was dealing with one quick Korean.

Just past mile seventeen, Sohn whizzed by Zabala, who was so stunned by Sohn's speed that he actually fell, which probably made the führer furious. For the last five miles, Sohn pulled away from the next closest competitor and won the gold medal. He became the first Olympic marathoner to run the race in less than two-and-a-half hours.

One of my favorite parts of my story—and I swear I didn't make it up—was when a Korean newspaper got angry about their star being forced to represent Japan. Just to make a point, they airbrushed the sunburst, Japan's national symbol, off Sohn's jersey on the front-page photo. The staff was thrown in prison and the newspaper was shut down for ten months as punishment.

But I bet it was worth it.

Word count check: 1,496. Closing time.

I never met my grandfather, but thinking about how tall he stood has inspired me. Beneath Sohn's

*Japanese jersey was a true Korean: proud of who
he was and determined to achieve.*

Finally I was finished. I'd told Sohn Kee Chung's story,
and he was one awesome Korean. If only our family connection were true.

I waited for the yahoo-I'm-done! exhilaration to hit
like it usually does when a paper's finished, but it didn't.
Sohn Kee Chung was proud and true to himself, but I
didn't feel that way.

I looked up. Dad had gone upstairs. I hit Save and
signed off. This wasn't the kind of document I wanted
Mom or Dad to see.

My sisters were still in the kitchen as I searched the
cupboard. Dad had let me skip dinner to finish the essay,
and now I was craving something cheesy with tomato
sauce.

"Did you two reach a truce?" I asked.

Only Sophie nodded, so I figured she ate the last
Popsicle. Gina was distracted, playing some sort of stack
'em game on the kitchen counter with the spice contain-
ers. She'd gotten eight of them on top of each other and
was attempting to add the dried rosemary to make it
nine, but it was wobbling.

"The leaning tower of flavor," I said in an accent just

like Nonno Calderaro's.

Gina giggled.

I poured a glass of orange juice and looked in the fridge, only to discover leftover pizza in the back, behind the margarine. *Yessss.* Heaven in tinfoil.

"C'mon, Gina and Sophie, bedtime. Brush your teeth," Dad called from upstairs. Gina got off her chair just as Sophie reached over and knocked the tower down. Plastic spice jars started rolling across the counter. Green flecks of oregano spilled everywhere.

"I saw you, Sophie, you brat!" Tears filled Gina's eyes.

Sophie grinned and then glanced at me.

"Why are you so mean?" I barked.

"Who says it was me?" she said, dashing out of the kitchen with guilt and Popsicle juice smeared across her face.

"That'll be five seventy-five," the pizza guy growled in a cartoon bulldog voice on Sunday afternoon. I handed him a ten-dollar bill and stuffed the change in my shorts pocket. Kelly was already walking to a booth in the back of the pizzeria.

"You didn't have to pay for me, Joseph," she said, poking a straw in her cup. She was drinking diet soda, though I doubt she weighed a hundred pounds. I can't stand diet anything.

The pizzeria was warm and crowded. A herd of Little Leaguers had just walked in. The smell of garlic floated in the air like it does when Mom's making her Bolognese sauce. It was almost four and I was starving, even though I'd eaten most of the popcorn at the movie theater.

Subtly, I watched how Kelly handled her pizza. Pizza-eating technique reveals a lot about a person. First Kelly placed a napkin on top and sopped up the grease. Then she pricked the cheese with a fork to release the heat. When she finally dug in, she took teensy bites and dabbed her chin with a napkin.

Me, the moment we sat down I reached for the Parmesan and the red pepper shaker and covered my pepperoni slice like sand on the desert. The more kick, the better. I'm convinced my spicy craving is genetic. Even in kindergarten I preferred ballpark chili dogs over plain franks.

Still, I didn't want to be a slob around Kelly. I was careful to not chew with my mouth open—which, according to Mom, is a bad habit of all us Calderaros.

We talked about how the movie creeped us both out. "My sister Sophie would have liked it," I said. "She loves getting scared to the brink of wetting her pants."

Kelly said she was the only child in her family.

I told her how I have five cousins on my dad's side, and six cousins—or cousins once removed, I get it mixed up—on my mom's side. "Italians have Rolodexes full of relatives," I added.

"Italians?"

"Yeah, most of my relatives on both sides moved to Florida. The warmer weather reminds them of Italy. We're the only family members who still own snow shovels."

Kelly started to speak, but then stopped. She seemed to be confused, about my being Italian, I guessed.

"I'm adopted." I shrugged, as if that explained it all.

"Really?" She looked surprised. Maybe she thought my dad was white and my mom was Asian. But I guess she never met my parents.

"Yup, I was born in Korea," I said, as though I could map the entire country. Under the booth I slapped my hands against my knees to the beat of "You're a Grand Old Flag."

Kelly put her drink down and perked up. "Do you know your story? I mean, who your parents were?"

"Oh, sure," I said. I don't know what made me say it.

Maybe to impress her. Or maybe because I felt dumb *not* knowing.

"So you've searched for your birth mother? I saw this Russian girl on a talk show who did that. She put a posting on a website and was reunited with her relatives."

"Sort of," I said. Inside my head I thought I heard that tiny angel Mom calls your conscience calling, "Liar, liar, pants on fire!"

Kelly stared at me wide-eyed, like a curious cat. I wanted her to think I was interesting, but I didn't really want to get into all this adoption stuff.

"Did you meet your birth mother?" she asked.

I shook my head no.

"Have you talked to her on the phone?"

"We're, uh, writing letters," I said. If only it were true. And now I felt like that tiny angel was smacking the inside of my brain, furious.

Just when I dreaded saying another word, one of the Little Leaguers ran past our table, tripped on his shoelace, and sent his paper plate flying.

Splat! His slice of meatball pizza landed cheese down on the linoleum, and he started wailing. I got up to hand the poor kid napkins. I hate hearing squirts cry.

Soon his mom took charge, and the boy calmed down.

Kelly and I sat quietly for a few minutes after that. I slurped my soda. It was empty, and I wanted a refill.

"I give you credit, Joseph. I don't know if I would have searched," Kelly said.

I looked up, surprised by her words. "Why not?"

"Because I like my life," she answered carefully, as if thinking it through. "You probably like yours, too. I'd be afraid of the skeletons in the closet, if you know what I mean."

I didn't. I wanted to know every single thing I could. What my birth parents looked like, what kind of jobs they had, their favorite foods and colors, even what songs they hummed in the shower. Knowing nothing is worse than knowing the truth. But I didn't tell that to Kelly. Mostly I wanted to change the subject.

"Be right back." I walked over to the counter and filled my soda to the top.

Since my plate was empty and Kelly's just had pizza crust, we went outside. It had started to rain lightly, and the sky was covered with dark cauliflower-shaped clouds.

"I'm supposed to meet my mom next door," she said, pointing to the florist. "She has to pick up centerpieces for a dinner for their restaurant suppliers tonight."

End-of-date rituals, can anything be more awkward?

I thought about kissing her, but it didn't feel right, what in the rain and with the Little Leaguers standing by the door eating Italian ices and staring at us. Besides, after all that crushed red pepper on my pizza, my breath might have set a class A fire on her lips.

"Let me know if you hear anything about your birth family, okay?" she said.

"Sure. So, um, do you wanna go out again sometime?"

"Maybe, but call me way ahead of time. The next couple of weeks are crazy busy. You know, commitments," she said, rolling her eyes.

As I nodded and waved good-bye, I tried to think of one thing in my life that qualified as a commitment. But I could only hear Mom yelling at me to hurry with that sack of towels before the Jiffy Wash closed.

I ran back to the CinemaPlex in the rain and sat on a bench inside, waiting for Dad. He'd taken Gina and Sophie to buy sneakers, and so I still had another twenty minutes to kill. I watched a few older guys standing in the ticket line with their arms around girls. It made me think about my afternoon. In Frankie-speak, I'd made contact with one of the hottest girls in school. We'd had fun together. She'd actually spoken the two victory words, "Call me."

Then why wasn't I having those heart-pounding,

firecracker-exploding feelings? My mind wasn't even on Kelly. Instead, my thoughts bounced from my essay about who I *wasn't*, to wondering about who I *was*. I needed to solve this MBA puzzle. Like why I always sneeze five times in a row. No one else I know sneezes more than three times. Or my constant craving for spicy food. Or my never-ending wondering about who came before me in that long line of ancestors Mrs. Peroutka talked about.

Maybe my birth mother sneezes in sets of five. Maybe my birth father loads his plate with hot peppers too. Who knows? Maybe some of my Korean relatives resisted the Japanese occupiers the way Sohn Kee Chung had.

I really wanted to know. No, I *needed* to know. There had to be a way to find out, I decided, even if the essay was already finished. I know Nash would help me. I'd tell him what Kelly said about that adopted Russian girl posting a note on the Internet. Maybe we could try that!

That's what was on my mind more than anything else. Even more than Kelly.

Finding Your Ki-bun

A few days later, I rang the doorbell at Nash's house less than ten minutes after he called. I licked my lips. They still tasted like the spice from the barbecue chips I'd wolfed down.

"You found something out about me, didn't you?" I asked as we ran upstairs.

"You bet I did," he said.

While we waited for the computer to boot up, Nash told me about his new lab partner in science. "I think she's Korean, Joseph, no kidding. She's really pretty and smart."

It had to be Ok-hee. I reminded him about Yongsu being the new kid in band and told him that was her brother. "The Hans bought the Jiffy Wash, near my mom's shop," I said.

"I'll carry towels for your mom whenever she wants," said Nash, "as long as Ok-hee's there."

Nash sounded slick, but I knew him well enough to know he probably acted shy around Ok-hee.

The computer screen finally lit up. With a click Nash called up a website called "Finding Your *Ki-bun*."

"What's *ki-bun*?" I asked.

"It sounds like good spirit, inner peace, that sort of thing. This website is for Korean adoptees tracing their family connections."

I wanted to do this, but my hands still trembled as I looked at the screen.

"You're not alone, Joseph. Check out these messages," Nash said.

The listings reminded me of newspaper classifieds, only sadder:

Please help me find my sister: We were left in the terminal at Kwangju Airport on July 16, 1978. I was three months old and my sister, Ji-Kun Lim, was four. She probably has an

96

American name now. I'd give anything to see her.

Looking for leads to my Korean past: I traveled from Seoul to Minneapolis in '86 when I was five months old. I have a small Mongolian spot birthmark on my left elbow. I want to meet someone I'm related to. I promise not to interfere with your life. I just want to know my other side.

Need answers: My wife and I recently had our first baby, and it's made me wonder about my early years. I was found in front of the American Embassy in Seoul on Christmas Eve, 1982. I was two years old and I had a tag on my wrist with my birth name, Oksu. Does anyone know my story?

Nash broke the silence. "Some stories, huh?"

"Do we know if any of these people found their families?" I asked.

Nash highlighted a message from a twenty-four-year-old graphic designer in Phoenix. "Look, Joseph. This lady made a connection."

Family reunion in Phoenix: My deepest thanks to those who cared enough to read my story. Because of you, I've been reunited with my father. The funny part is that we look alike, speak alike, and even laugh alike! He will be coming to Arizona to visit next month.

I tried to imagine meeting a Korean relative for the first time. Somebody who looks just like me. Would I crack a joke? Would my voice quiver when I introduced myself? Would we hug?

Nash roamed around the website. He clicked the e-form for making a posting and waited for me to say something.

Then Chicken Calderaro started clucking. "I don't know what I'm getting into, Nash. Maybe this was a bad idea. What do you think?"

"I'd want to know my story. But what do *you* want?"

I stared at the computer screen and reread the message from the lady in Phoenix. Then I looked right at Nash. "I want to know," I finally replied.

"Then let's go for it."

Well, if I was going to search, my message was going to get noticed. "I'll talk, you type, Nash. Here's the lead-in:

New Jersey Italian Stallion looking for Korean connection: Clue lies in the basket a little old lady found at the Pusan police station in May fourteen years ago. . . .

Too Tangled for Spider-Man

"Why would anyone name a band Chicago?" Steve whispered from the bass drum.

"It sure beats calling it Hoboken," I said.

"Hey, watch what you say, Joseph. I was *born* in Hoboken."

"Yeah, I can tell by your bad breath," I shot back, and we both laughed.

Mrs. Athena had summoned us for a special early-bird session. We were working on "Saturday in the Park," a seventies hit that leaned heavy on drums and trumpet. This was supposed to be the kickoff song for the concert, but Mrs. Athena said it needed some TLC. Personally, I think it was those can't-reed-to-save-their-lives clarinets that needed help, not the rest of us.

Jeff was absent, so Steve and I were multitasking most of the percussion instruments. It felt like circuit training—intervals of banging mallets on the xylophone, whacking the timpani, and then running to the snare, all while handling cymbals, too. Here's one of many band myths: people think cymbals are the musical equivalent of wrecking balls that crash into each other randomly, but there's more of an art to it than that. If you play them right, cymbals should slice each other like you're cutting cheese off a pizza.

I sang along as I banged out the beat. Dad owns *Chicago's Greatest Hits*, so I knew all the lyrics.

"Yo, Joseph."

"What, Steve?"

"When do you think Mrs. Peroutka will hand back our essays? The odds are fifty-fifty that I'm going to summer school, and I *really* need a decent grade in social studies."

"Should be any day now." I wanted to get a good grade on the essay too. That way I'd make high honor roll again. Right now my grade was a B+. But thinking about my essay got my stomach fluttering. What if Mrs.

Peroutka caught me in the act of re-creating history? I actually lost my place worrying about it and came in a half measure late on xylophone.

"Everything okay, Joseph?" Mrs. Athena called. She never misses a beat.

"Any day now" turned out to be the next day.

"Welcome, class," Mrs. Peroutka cawed when we filed into social studies.

There was no mistaking me for Sammy Sunshine that Friday morning. My déjà-vu dream returned again last night, and this time it felt more like a nightmare. I was back walking on that dirt road and pulling that wagon, only this time I was by myself. It was dark and pouring rain, and I could hear animal noises in the distance. I woke up in a cold sweat.

Then, after another burned Pop-Tart breakfast, a bird pooped on my Yankees cap at the bus stop, and someone stole my shorts from my gym locker. In the words of a true Korean, I was not feeling good *ki-bun*.

But Mrs. Peroutka was all smiles as she stood in front of the classroom. She was wearing a shiny green dress that made her look like a waxed lime.

The bell rang, and she picked up a stack of papers.

"I'm delighted to return your essays," she began. "I was impressed by the quality of your writing and moved by the emotion you all conveyed in your stories."

Twenty-five deep sighs of relief followed.

"Unlike my fifth and sixth periods, no one here earned less than a B. Each of you shared fascinating details about your family's legacy."

Phew. I had at least a B. That was decent, but I wanted an A.

I glanced at Steve. He flashed me a metal mouth smile. That B meant a get-out-of-summer-school-free pass for him.

Mrs. Peroutka walked from desk to desk, placing the papers facedown. "Before you read my comments, I want to say something that I didn't tell you earlier, mostly because I hoped you'd write from the heart."

Then she explained that she had the difficult task of selecting what she considered to be the finest essay from all her students. That essay would be entered in a national essay contest that complemented our heritage unit. The decision was especially difficult, she said, because of all the wonderful writing.

"I can only submit one essay for the contest, but I intend to display all of them at the Celebrating Our

Heritage Night next week. And I was hoping that some of you would read excerpts for your families that night as well."

No thanks, I thought. I'll pass on that ordeal.

Mrs. Peroutka's eyes twinkled behind her glasses. "I'm pleased to announce that I've selected Joseph Calderaro's inspiring story about his grandfather Sohn Kee Chung, the Olympian."

Gulp. *Me? The winner?* My armpits got sweaty like I'd been doing pull-ups. My cheeks felt like they'd been slapped. And dread burned in my throat like I'd swallowed too many jalapeño peppers.

The class was silent, and then everyone started clapping.

"Way to go, Timpani Man!" Steve cheered.

"An Olympian?" Robyn called out. "I've suffered through the mile run with you. Who knew you had running genes?"

Mrs. Peroutka kept smiling, but I couldn't even look her in the eye. I couldn't say a word, even though everyone stared at me, expecting to hear something. My stomach convulsed like I'd drunk a milkshake without taking a lactose pill.

Lucky for me, the fire alarm sounded off and we filed out of class. Usually fire drills are the high point of a day, total time wasters, but not today. As the kids and teachers stood around waiting by the tennis courts, I avoided eye contact with everybody, as if I had a giant zit on my nose.

"You rock, Joseph. You must be way proud of your grandfather," Robyn whispered while Mrs. Peroutka counted heads.

"Thanks," I said, sheepishly.

"And I thought it was impressive that my uncle won five thousand dollars at the Monmouth Park Racetrack. Speaking of horses, why did the horse go behind the tree?" she asked.

I shrugged.

"To change his jockeys!"

Robyn waited for me to laugh or come back with my own lame joke. But I stood quietly, pretending to take the fire drill seriously, even though we were allowed to talk now.

But I couldn't pretend I didn't hear my name being called—loud.

"Congrats, Joseph!" Kelly yelled across the crowd of kids talking.

I nodded. What else could I do? Everyone looked at me, probably wondering what I'd done and why a girl like Kelly cared.

The assistant principal gave the hand signal that the

fire drill was over, and everyone funneled back into school. Fate had it that my class reached the door just as Kelly's did.

"I just heard your essay won, and that you wrote about your grandfather, the Olympic star. Wow! Did your Korean family tell you all that?"

I stared at the back of the head in front of me. "Sort of."

"A gold-medal-winning relative. That is sooo cool," she said.

"Thanks." *If only you knew,* I thought.

"Well, if you feel like celebrating, I'm going miniature golfing next Saturday with a bunch of my friends. You can come if you want."

Kelly was inviting *me* to hang out with *her*? Meanwhile I felt like Chicken Little with the sky falling down.

"Maybe" is all I could manage to squeak in return.

On the way home I kept thinking about ways to get out of this mess. Confess over dinner? No way. Mom and Dad would lose it right between the antipasto and the main course. Worse, I could almost feel the weight of their disappointment already, since dishonesty is a big no-no for us Calderaros. Ask Mrs. Peroutka to withdraw me as the winner? Then she'd want to know why. Do nothing? Nah, I couldn't live with my sleazy secret forever. I'd be like that eighties rock group Aunt Foxy told me about, Milli Vanilli. She said they made millions of dollars by lip-synching other people's music, but eventually the truth came out and they had to face their *own* music.

On top of all that, I was feeling guilty—about forgery, history tampering, or whatever crime it was that I'd committed. Dad always bragged that I was a straight-as-a-ruler kid. It used to be true.

As I walked up the driveway, this random quote popped into my head. It was something our teacher made us memorize last year after we finished reading Shakespeare's *Othello*:

> *"Oh, what a tangled web we weave,*
> *When first we practice to deceive!"*

Even Spider-Man couldn't untangle this web.

Who Cares About Mark Twain?

The house stank like broccoli when I walked in the doorway. Dad was in the kitchen wearing the chef's apron Mom had given him for Father's Day. He was home early, he said, because a customer had cancelled at the last minute. Usually that made Dad furious, but today he seemed cheery, like maybe he didn't want to be up on a ladder with dirty water running down his forearms, washing some doctor's windows on a Friday afternoon.

He was standing over a pot of boiling water. "Tonight we feast on linguini with creamy broccoli sauce, salad drizzled with balsamic vinegar, and bruschetta. *Deliziosa cena!*"

Dad doesn't cook all that often, but when he does, he goes all out. Opera music was playing in the family room. Blasting, actually.

"Want a sample?" he asked as he stirred the sauce.

"Maybe later." At that moment no meal in the world could get me drooling. My stomach still felt like someone was wringing it out with bare hands.

I knew I had to level about what I'd done.

One on one is easier than two on one when you're breaking bad news to parents. I decided to tell Dad first and Mom later, when she got home.

I pulled a kitchen stool close to the counter, where Dad was chopping onions and garlic, and sat down.

"I did something you're not going to be happy about, Dad." I spoke loudly over the mezzo-soprano.

Dad stopped chopping.

"Remember that essay I had to write about my ancestors?"

He nodded.

"Well, I didn't know anything about my Korean relatives, so I sort of made up a story about my grandfather . . . in Korea."

"What do you mean, 'made it up'?"

"I wrote about this Korean runner named Sohn Kee Chung who won a gold medal at the Olympics in 1936. That part's true. Thing is, I said he was my grandfather. And now my essay won a contest."

The timer went off, and Dad carried the pot over to the sink and drained the pasta. He was shaking his head while the steam rose from the colander.

"You're an honest kid, Joseph. Why'd you do that? You could have written ten pages about Grandpa Calderaro and his tailor shop."

"I told you already, it's supposed to be about *my* heritage, not yours."

"You know what Mark Twain said about telling the truth?" Dad asked.

Of course I didn't give a rat's poop about what Mark Twain said in whatever classic Dad had read. I said nothing.

"He said, 'If you tell the truth, you don't have to remember anything.'"

"Then how come the telling part doesn't work when it comes to me being adopted!" I yelled.

Dad's face tensed up, and the Mad Meter started pulsing fast like the maracas in "La Cucaracha." "You think being adopted gives you the right to disrespect me?"

Respect had nothing to do with it. "You don't under-

stand and you won't talk about anything." I shook my head and crossed my arms.

"How can you say this isn't your *real* family? I've tried to be the best father I can be for you, Joseph. That's what *I* understand. Every day I go out there and break my back for you and your sisters. So does your mother. *That's* family!"

Dad stomped over to the family room and turned the music down. Meanwhile, his temper rose way up with his voice.

"I've never been dishonest about your adoption, Joseph. The truth is, Mom and I know very little. That's how it is in Korea!"

I could yell too. "It's not just about what you know, Dad! Why can't you deal with who I am? I couldn't count on you to help me write one lousy essay. Last time I checked, being adopted wasn't a crime, but you sure act like it is!"

I stormed upstairs and slammed my bedroom door. Then I opened my socks-and-underwear drawer, grabbed the box with the *corno*, and threw it across the room. *Whack*! It hit my Amazing Spider-Man poster and fell behind my bed. The poster came crashing down behind it. Even the coolest superhero had collapsed from the stress of living in this house.

I walked to Nash's house, but nobody was home. Then I headed toward Shear Impressions, but turned around. I didn't want to face Mom yet.

Somehow I ended up at the Jiffy Wash.

"Yongsu's out back," Mrs. Han said, carrying a stack of shirts and jerking her head in that direction.

I was heading for the door when Ok-hee walked in.

"Mrs. Peroutka told my class that you won the essay contest," she said with an unexpected smile.

I nodded, wishing I could disappear between the hangers of shrink-wrapped clothes.

"My essay was about my great-grandmother in Taegu. She made beautiful mother-of-pearl jewelry boxes. What did you write about?"

"Miscellaneous Korean stuff," I said. Ok-hee was finally acting normal, not superior, but this topic was off limits.

A customer walked in with a blanket in her arms, and Mrs. Han turned around.

"I'd like to read your essay," Ok-hee said.

Double geez.

"Sorry, left it at school. See ya!" I said, tearing out of there faster than the Flash, the quickest dude in the comic book universe.

Yongsu was in the parking lot, fooling around with an old skateboard he'd found next to the Dumpster. He got us root beers from the fridge, and we hung out for a while. We didn't talk about school, Korea, or anything, really. I just watched him try skateboard jumps and wipe out a lot. He took so many spills that we started counting them and laughing.

I almost forgot about that lousy essay. Almost.

Pouring on the Guilt Gravy

"You're in big trouble, Joseph. Mommy and Daddy are talking about you on the patio, and Daddy's Mad Meter is on," Gina announced in her Channel Five reporter voice. Frazer was at her side, drooling as usual.

I'd missed Dad's gourmet feast, though I noticed a foil-covered plate was left for me on the stove. The kitchen smelled more like garlic than broccoli now. It made me realize how hungry I was.

I poured myself a glass of orange juice. Then I zapped my dinner in the microwave. Gina came over and parked herself next to me at the kitchen table with a bag of Oreos and a glass of milk. Eeyore sat next to her on the chair.

"Where's Sophie?" I asked as I sprinkled red pepper on my steaming linguini.

"At Kaylie Heinz's bowling party. She always gets invited to birthday parties and I don't."

"Kaylie plays soccer with Sophie, that's why," I said.

"Or maybe it's because kids think I'm a double-squared dork." She sulked, her eyes looking down from behind her glasses.

Gina kept pulling apart her Oreos, scooping the filling out with her pinkie fingernail, licking the chocolate shells, and clumping them in a pile. It looked nasty, but I have to admit I prefer the cream to those dry Frisbees too.

I started to tune Gina's whining out after a while. Here I was facing an academic felony, and she was carrying on about her lagging second-grade social life. Big deal.

"I wish I were adopted like you, Joseph," Gina said.

That got my attention. "Why?"

"'Cause it makes you special. Everyone compares me to Sophie. We learned about antonyms in school today, like fat and skinny, hot and cold. Sophie and me, we're twin antonyms. She's chocolate chip cookie dough ice cream and I'm boring vanilla."

"You wouldn't want to be the same as Sophie," I said.

"Yes I would." She grabbed another Oreo and banged it on the kitchen table. It broke and fell to the floor. "See? Even eating cookies is a tragedy for me!"

I stifled a laugh. "Having clone Sophies would be like sticking two fighting fish in the same tank. Besides, different doesn't mean you're not as good."

She kept shaking her head. I knew that whatever I said was going to sound lame, like a parent insisting "you tried your best" after you got cut from the team.

Hadn't I felt second-rate when Gina and Sophie were born? I remember looking down at their cute little faces in their matching wicker bassinets, wondering if Mom and Dad would still call *me* their baby. Nonna Sculletti said the twins had Sculletti noses, and Nonna Calderaro called them the picture of Dad. Of course, no one said any of that about me.

As I got up to refill my glass, I thought about an Italian saying Nonna Calderaro uses: Only the spoon knows what's stirring the pot. I had adoption stuff on my mind, and meanwhile, Gina, the cutest tadpole from Mom and Dad's own gene pool, had her own identity crisis. Who knew?

"Okay, here's something that makes Gina Calderaro special in my book. Nobody sings 'Hakuna Matata' like you. Keep it up, and you just might get into Disney University."

A smile slowly crossed Gina's face. "I love singing. You really think I'm good?"

"You bet your donkey." I tugged on Eeyore's floppy ear.

"There's no such place as Disney University, Joseph," she said with her mouth showing mashed cookie.

"Says who? I read about this geeky guy who graduated first in his class from Disney U. He wore glasses and had a twin, too. Now he's got the lead on Broadway in *Beauty and the Beast*."

Gina was giggling now, her long hair swinging forward and almost falling into her glass of milk.

"He's a lot hairier than you, but you've got time." I swiped the last unlicked Oreo.

"Mommy said the Y is offering kids' singing lessons starting this month. She says she'll sign me up if I promise not to change my mind like last year, after she paid."

"Go for it, Gina," I said.

Then I saw Mom and Dad stand up from their patio chairs. They looked as if they were coming my way, so I headed out of their way. Upstairs.

I was in bed reading an oldie-but-goodie comic, "The Revenge of the Green Goblin," when I heard the knock. Actually it was more like *knock-knock-BANG!*, which could only mean one thing: Mom was on a rampage.

Since dinner I'd felt like a gunfighter readying myself for a showdown. Not only was the waiting stressful, but I had indigestion from the creamy broccoli sauce.

Mom barged in. "Talk to me about this essay," she demanded, her arms crossed over her checkered nightgown.

"Didn't Dad give you the *Reader's Digest* version?"

She grabbed a sock off the floor and flung it at me. "What were you thinking, making up that story?"

Mom started pacing, which isn't easy to do in my room. Gina and Sophie have the longer room, which gives Mom more space. Then she started pouring on the guilt gravy—how she's never hidden anything from me, how she's always tried to be truthful, and how come I wasn't honest in my essay.

"What, we embarrass you, is that it?" she shouted, her hands flailing up and down like railroad crossing signs. "Your father is so upset, he barely touched his dinner— and he made it!"

"I didn't mean to hurt anyone, Mom."

She kept shaking her head. Without makeup her skin looked chalky against her dark eyes, and that made her seem even madder.

"It was a dumb mistake. I'm sorry." I stared at my stack of comic books underneath the nightstand.

"You know what plagiarism is, Joseph?"

"This isn't plagiarism, Mom. I wrote the story myself. I didn't copy it."

"But that man wasn't your grandfather. You stole him from a book! Your father and I decided that for lying, you're sentenced to a weekend of yard work. No going over to Nash's house, no TV, and no video games."

I pouted my lips, but actually I'd gotten off easy. Maybe Mom was going light on me because she knew how bad I'd get hassled at school. They might suspend me, or even expel me. Then I'd have to go to a reform school with psychopaths who'd cut off my ears if I didn't hand over my lunch money.

Mom walked toward the door, but then she stopped. "Lying, trouble in school—this isn't like you, Joseph. You're adopted, and that's perfectly fine. Why didn't you tell the truth?" She rubbed her eyelids with her fingertips.

"I don't *know* the whole truth, Mom," I said. "Sometimes I look in the mirror and wish I knew more about the kid staring back. It's nothing against you and Dad."

"Mom! We're out of toothpaste!" Gina yelled from the bathroom.

"You want to know more about yourself, being Korean? Is that it?"

I nodded and thought about the Internet posting. Wondered if I should've told Mom about that too.

"I understand that, honey. And deep down, your father can too. He has a heart bigger than the ladder on his truck, but he's pigheaded. You're his oldest and only son, Joseph. I swear, sometimes he forgets that you're adopted."

"It's not like I got a vote," I said.

"Joseph, adopting you was one of the most wonderful days of my life. Your father's, too," she said, and her eyes filled up with tears. My hands trembled against my comic book.

"Your father . . . well, I know he's hard to talk to sometimes, but that doesn't mean he doesn't accept you for who you are," she added.

"But you're speaking *for* him, Mom. Dad never talks like that, and that's part of the problem."

"Well, maybe I am speaking for him, but after being married to your father for twenty years, I know his every thought."

"Will someone help me? I need toothpaste!" Gina shouted like she was drowning.

"Stop yelling! Geez Louise, it's on the shelf under the sink," Mom snapped. Then she flipped on my night-light.

"I wish you'd talked to me about your essay," she said, a bit softer. "We could've figured something out together. I would've tried to help."

"Will you talk to Mrs. Peroutka for me?" I asked. "Explain how I'm adopted so we can fix this?"

"Joseph, my job isn't to fix everything for you. My job is to help you deal with life's messy parts. I'm sorry, but you'll have to talk to your teacher yourself."

Ugh. Just thinking about walking into Mrs. Peroutka's class made my stomach hurt again. Facing her. Facing everyone. Like how Susan Amber must have felt last year when she got caught rigging the yearbook's "cutest smile" vote for herself.

"Capisce?" Mom asked.

I nodded. *"Capisce."*

"No more stolen relatives. Go see your teacher on Monday morning with a big shovel and dig yourself out of this hole."

Essaygate

Forty-eight hours without TV and video games felt like cruel and unusual punishment. And what made it even worse was dreading Monday, my day of reckoning. I kept rehearsing what I'd tell Mrs. Peroutka. I even had a nightmare that after I'd fessed up, a CNN reporter stuck a microphone in my face and shouted, "So, was being adopted what corrupted you?"

After social studies ended, I waited until the last kid left the room to come clean. Mrs. Peroutka was erasing the chalkboard when I approached her. Shoving my sweaty hands in my shorts pockets, I plunged right into my confession of how I made up the Sohn Kee Chung story.

When I finished, I put on my sorry face I use when I lose the house key or forget to throw the clothes in the dryer for Mom. Mrs. Peroutka was ancient and demanding, but I could tell she cared about her students. I didn't like disappointing her.

But Mrs. Peroutka didn't raise her eyebrows or reach for her red pen and grade book. Instead she barraged me with a bunch of deep questions.

"Out of all the famous Koreans to be related to, why did you choose Sohn Kee Chung?" she asked.

I shrugged my shoulders. "He seemed brave, a cross between a jock and a rebel."

"How so?"

I told her about Korea's occupation, and how Sohn Kee Chung had to run wearing a Japanese jersey. "Some Koreans were upset with him for running. Like it was *his* fault that his country got invaded."

"That was a difficult time for Korea," she said, nodding.

"But even with the Japanese threatening him, he never missed a chance to tell reporters that Korea was his mother country," I added.

Mrs. Peroutka kept asking questions, and I had

answers. I was surprised how much I remembered from that library book.

Then she kicked in with the self-examining stuff. "Why do you think I assigned this essay, Joseph?"

"So someone from our school can win the contest?" I was joking, sort of.

She frowned, and I wished I'd zipped my lips.

"I want my students to spend time thinking about their families, living and deceased. Sometimes it feels like the here and now is all that matters, but we have legacies that help shape who we are. I think about my relatives on my mother's side. They were Polish Jews who came to America to escape persecution. They never took for granted the freedom they made a difficult journey to discover."

She paused, then added, "Did this essay make you curious about yourself?"

I nodded. It had made me curious enough to query the world about my birth via the Internet. But it had also unleashed epic problems, kind of like the demons inside Pandora's box.

Mrs. Peroutka continued probing. "In what way?"

"It just added to it. Being adopted makes me wonder about stuff anyway. I wish I could *stop* wondering."

"Good for you that you wonder, Joseph. It's a sign of a

maturing mind," she said with a smile. Suddenly I had a feeling that I wouldn't be spending the afternoon in detention after all.

I glanced out the door of the classroom. Yongsu passed by and waved wildly.

"Joseph, it sounds as if you can't write about your biological lineage right now. But it seems to me that you *are* quite reflective about your past, your family, and your origins. And I bet you've already started discovering some things about what it means to be Korean."

The one-minute-until-you're-late bell rang, but Mrs. Peroutka kept going. "I think the circumstances justify my giving you a second chance. Your makeup essay can address your ethnicity and other aspects of your identity—including your adoption, if you want. It doesn't have to be about your blood relations," she added, wiping chalk from her hands.

"Thanks, Mrs. Peroutka," I said. "I mean . . . well, for listening to me."

I owed her that. She'd given me a do-over when she could've sliced the you-flunk guillotine on my neck.

"One more thing, Joseph," she called as I started to leave. "Your revised essay is due next Tuesday. And while I enjoy your storytelling, I expect nonfiction this time."

• • •

I stood in the express checkout lane that night feeling half-and-half, like the cream Mom sent me in for. I felt half relieved that I'd made my confession, and half crummy that the truth was out. Rumors were spreading at school that I'd bought an essay over the Internet and tried to pass it off as my own. As if. We're not even *online* at my house.

Just as I put the cream, bread, and Capicola ham on the conveyor belt, Kelly walked into the supermarket.

For a second I pretended not to see her, what with all the talk going around about me. But no, Kelly and I were friends. She'd understand. So as soon as I paid the cashier, I walked over to her in the floral section. We hadn't talked since she'd asked me about playing miniature golf, and I wondered if we were still on.

I tapped her on the shoulder. "What's up, MVP?"

"Nothing," she snapped back without looking at me. Her arms were crossed, and she kept staring at the bouquets on the $5.99 display rack.

"Whatsamatta?" I rested the grocery bag on the floor.

"You're a big liar, that's what. I heard about your fake essay. And to think I fell for your 'I'm adopted and writing letters to my birth family' story."

She kept staring at those flowers. I felt like jumping up on the display just to get her attention.

Dad told me once how President Nixon lied and had to leave the White House in disgrace because of a scandal called Watergate. Looking at Kelly's scowling face, I realized that I was caught up in Essaygate.

"I wasn't lying, Kelly. I *am* adopted. And if I wanted to impress you, I would've come up with a much better story. Trust me."

No response.

"Listen, I couldn't write the essay because I don't know my birth family," I said, staring down at my sneakers. "My parents don't know anything either, and I panicked."

Finally she looked at me. "You told me you were writing back and forth with your family in Korea," she said.

"I want to . . . I mean, I'm going to. It's complicated."

"I don't respect dishonest people," she declared. And she walked past me so fast that I felt a breeze.

That was when I felt my blood really starting to boil, as Aunt Foxy says. How dare she suggest I'm dishonest! Last year I found five dollars wedged in the seat on the school bus and I turned it in to the bus driver.

Besides, Kelly didn't have a clue what it was like being adopted. Not a clue.

I marched right up beside her, next to a giant cactus. "Know what, Kelly? I don't respect golden girls who rush to judge others without checking the facts. And by the way, I'll pass on miniature golf this weekend. I've got commitments." Then I picked up the grocery bag and headed toward the automatic exit door.

Like Dad, I mixed metaphors, but I got my point across.

Then the door shut behind me. On Kelly and any wish I had for us to go to the Farewell Formal together.

Comic Relief

Nash and I locked our bikes in front of the comic book store. It was drizzling and windy and we knew we were nuts to have ridden into town, but we both needed a pick-me-up. Nash wanted to join a summer roller hockey league, but his mom wouldn't let him because of his migraines. And last night had been the Celebrating Our Heritage Night at school, but my family hadn't gone. Mrs. Peroutka encouraged me to go, but I couldn't get past Essaygate. Everyone would have whispered and stared at me like I was an ex-con.

All wasn't doomed, however. Today was the last

Wednesday of the month, which meant good news for diehard comic fans: the latest *Amazing Spider-Man* would be on the shelf!

I wiped rain off my forehead as Nash opened the door to Nothing But Comics. It felt warm inside and it smelled musty, as usual. No one was there but Corn Head, the guy who owns the store. He's got choppy dark hair, but he bleaches the tips yellow like corn kernels. For five years Nash and I have been coming to this store, and I doubt Corn Head has ever said more than ten words to us. Me, if I owned a comic book store—and I just might someday—I'd yack for hours with my customers. And I'd copycat the bookstore chains and open up a Superhero Café right inside. Only I'd skip the lattes and biscotti and sell barbecue potato chips, candy bars, and sodas. Nothing else goes better with a crisp new comic.

Nash and I walked straight to the Marvel section, and I grabbed "Amazing Spider-Man #788." He picked up the latest "Wolverine," then put it back again.

"Just this," I said, handing the comic and my money to Corn Head. Then I waited for Nash. I had a feeling he was low on cash, so I tried to give him my change, but he shook his head no.

"Take it. It's not like I've got a girl to spend it on," I said.

I knew Nash wanted the comic. The cover had an awesome hologram of Wolverine with his claws wrapped around Magneto's neck, on top of a skyscraper.

"Thanks. I'll pay you back, promise," he assured me.

"Just think of it as a cash advance for my search fee," I said.

We crossed the street and went to Salvo's Corner Store. I was drooling for some chocolate, and we still had money to blow.

"So what happened with Kelly?" Nash asked as we walked to the back of the store.

"She turned on me after Essaygate. It hurt her reputation to hang out with a pond-scum plagiarizer," I said.

Nash pulled open the refrigerator case and grabbed two root beers off the shelf. "What does Kelly Gerken know? The only subject she's an expert on is herself," he said, shaking his head.

The rain was pouring down in buckets when left the store, so we waited under the awning for it to stop. We watched the street get soaked, drinking our root beers and splitting a Baby Ruth bar.

"Talk about bad luck, Joseph. I finally got my chance to talk with Ok-hee the other day because we'd finished our lab before the rest of the class. But wouldn't you know, I get called down to the office. My mom signed me out of school for *another* neurologist appointment."

"That stinks worse than skunk juice!"

He nodded. "My mom's *obsessed* with my migraines. She's dragged me to three doctors so far this month."

"Can't they just give you something to stop them?" I asked.

Nash shrugged. "It's not that easy. My mom still thinks sports trigger the headaches since they started last year during hockey. But I read that sometimes it's diet. I've started keeping track of what I eat and drink every day to figure it out myself."

"You should rig your journal to prove homework causes migraines," I suggested.

"Hmm," Nash said, rubbing his chin.

We both laughed.

As we walked back toward our bikes, Nash told me he'd been checking my posting every day. "One response came in yesterday, but the guy sounded messed up. He wrote that he was your long-lost brother, and that he wanted to reunite on a live talk show."

"What makes you so sure he's a fake?"

"He wanted a hundred bucks first."

"Good thing I've got you looking out for me," I said. But inside I didn't feel good about the search. Or hopeful. "Nothing's going to turn up, Nash. I'm starting to think the adoption agency just pulled me out of a deep dark hole. Abracadabra, one Korean kid."

"We've got a chance. Your posting had more details than some of the others. It just takes time."

Maybe it was hearing about the adoption scam artist. Or maybe it was talking about the essay and Kelly. But suddenly I felt empty—like the soda bottle in my hand.

Yet it was like Nash could read my mind, because quick as lightning, he hopped on his bike and shouted, "I should write in your posting how your best friend can kick your butt in a bike race!"

And off he flew, racing down the street, zigzagging from one side to the other.

My down-in-the-dumps mood disappeared faster than that Baby Ruth bar. Challenging Joseph Calderaro is risky business. I pushed up the kickstand, jumped on my seat, and took off.

Pedaling like a Tour de France champion, I whizzed by Nash, my face and hair dripping wet. I knew that his mom wouldn't be happy with our racing, but Nash sure looked headache free to me.

"You gotta do better than that, Wolverine Wannabe!" I shouted out to him, pedaling furiously with my back to the wind.

Korean Culture 101

"Joseph, telephone!" Sophie shouted that night. I jumped up from my desk, thrilled with an excuse to stop working on Version Two of The Essay That Destroyed My Life.

The voice on the phone was so squeaky that, at first, I thought it was a girl.

"Do you want to come to my house for dinner tomorrow night?" Yongsu asked. "My mom's making *bulgogi*, and we can watch a Jackie Chan video afterward."

"*Bulgogi?*"

"Bul-go-gi," he answered slowly. "It means 'fire meat.'"

"Oh, it's spicy?"

"It's thin beef strips that get marinated and grilled. Tastes a little spicy and a little sweet."

Yum. "Does your mom know you're asking me?"

"Sure," he said. "Your mom permed my mom's hair yesterday."

Aha. Maria Calderaro's manicured fingers were meddling again. She must have come up with this plan as a way for me to learn about Korea. I could just hear her bribing Mrs. Han: "You give my kid the Korean lowdown and I'll perm you for half price."

But I wasn't sure about this dinner. Mrs. Han still treated me like the poster boy for Korea's shame, and the Hans' house was the real deal. How could I enjoy *bulgogi* while feeling like a Korean knucklehead?

Well, I had no plans anyway. Nash was going to visit his sister at college. And Frankie was grounded all week for using his mom's cell phone to interview Farewell Formal date candidates.

Besides, nobody smashes heads and breaks bones better than Jackie Chan. And I *was* curious about the Hans.

"Sure, I can come, Yongsu. Just make sure it's one of

the *old* Jackie Chan movies."

"Oh yeah," he said. "He kicks and punches way better in the old ones."

Garlic and soy sauce. Yongsu opened the front door and that's all I smelled. Our house smells garlicky too, but more like garlic and tomato.

I followed Yongsu into the Hans' narrow kitchen. Mrs. Han was standing near the stove, scooping rice out of a pot. The walls were covered with orange wallpaper. Above the kitchen table was a painting of two Korean men, sitting cross-legged, playing instruments that looked like coconuts strung together. Asian drummers, I thought. Like me.

"Hello, Mrs. Han." I spoke politely, bowing like Yongsu did when he greeted his dad. I handed her the wrapped pignoli cookies that Mom picked up from Randazzo's.

She smiled, then said something that I didn't understand.

"Excuse me?" I asked.

"*Gamsa hamnida*, thank you."

I smiled.

"You say, 'you're welcome,' *ch'onman-eyo*. You try."

I did, but those sounds didn't roll off my tongue as smoothly. I felt like a toddler taking his first steps. Then

Mrs. Han spoke to Yongsu in Korean. I could tell it was about me.

Yongsu nudged my elbow. He pointed to my sneakers. "We don't wear shoes in the house."

I looked in the hallway. A row of shoes rested against the wall.

Duh. A real Korean would have known that.

Full of dread, I untied my sneakers. One of my socks had a huge hole in the heel, and the other looked more brown than white.

Classical music floated from the room off the kitchen. It sounded like a song we'd played once in a concert. I peeked over the half wall and saw Ok-hee curled up on the couch, reading.

"Ah, Vivaldi. I know him well," I called to her as I followed Yongsu into the wood-paneled room.

"Lucky guess," she answered without even looking up from *Teen People*. Mom always keeps a copy of that magazine in the shop. It didn't exactly fit Ok-hee's brilliant babe image, but I guess smart girls just want to be girls too.

"You must be who I'm playing the duet with for the moving-up ceremony," Ok-hee added casually.

"Mistaken identity," I said. "That would be Steve. I'm the gifted drummer with the solo."

137

Ok-hee laughed.

This seemed like a good time to put a word in for Nash.

"Do you know my friend Pete Nash?" I asked. "He plays trumpet."

She nodded. "We're lab partners in science. He's kind of quiet."

"He just seems shy until you get to know him. Get him out of that academic dungeon and he really opens up. He's a computer whiz and a great hockey player, too."

"I didn't know he played hockey."

"Yeah, well, there's a lot more to Nash than his freckles."

Yongsu nudged me. "C'mon, let's start *Dragons Forever* before dinner."

Dragons Forever? That's my all-time favorite Jackie Chan movie. "Let's do it. What could be better than Jackie's jump in the last fight scene?"

An hour later we gathered for dinner around a card table that Mrs. Han had covered with a crocheted table-cloth. I sat next to Yongsu, across from Ok-hee.

Mr. Han was the last to join us. He'd come home from work later than Mrs. Han. I noticed that nobody touched a thing, not even a water glass, until he was ready.

Before we started eating, Mr. Han turned to me. "Joseph, your mother tells us you need to learn about Korea. You ask us any questions you want."

I nodded, but I felt insulted. Was this supposed to be dinner, or an educate-the-confused-Korean mission? No way would I act like that. Korean blood flowed through my veins just like theirs.

Mrs. Han walked from seat to seat, scooping mounds of sticky white rice into small bowls near our plates. Then she placed a large bowl next to the meat platter. It was full of vegetables covered in an orangey sauce, and it smelled like rotten fish.

Yongsu must have seen me staring. "That's kimchi," he explained.

"I know," I said, but I didn't really, although I'd read about Sohn Kee Chung's family eating kimchi.

There were no knives or forks, but chopsticks lay next to each folded napkin. Mine were wooden. The Hans' were silver.

Everyone dug in after Mrs. Han sat down, but I hesitated. Whenever I use chopsticks in a restaurant, the floor beneath my chair collects more food debris than the Meadowlands Arena after a rock concert.

Out of the corner of my eye, I watched Yongsu eat. He quickly picked bits of food off his plate with his chopsticks as if they were pinchers extending from his fingers. But my chopsticks had a mind of their own. The harder I squeezed, the wider they swung apart. Halfway to my mouth, most of the food fell. So I tried pushing them together and using them like a shovel, but you don't shovel much rice with chopsticks.

Without a word Mrs. Han came over, took one of my chopsticks, placed it against the crook of my thumb, and wrapped my middle and ring fingers around it like it was a pen. Then she tucked the other between the tip of my thumb and my pointer finger.

"Hold the bottom one still," she explained, pivoting the top one like a lever.

I pressed too hard and the bottom stick wobbled.

"Relax your hands," she added, adjusting my grip.

I tried again with lame results. And again, only this time I speared a piece of *bulgogi*.

Mrs. Han readjusted my fingers. "No poking with chopsticks. You can do it, Joseph."

Eyeing a big clump of rice in my bowl, I tried her technique, holding the bottom chopstick steady. This time the rice made it all the way to my mouth. I grinned, savoring the hard-earned taste.

"Thanks, the chopsticks are different at my house," I said, just as—*plop!*—a piece of *bulgogi* slipped between my chopsticks and into my water glass.

Everyone laughed, even me. It *was* funny.

"Try some kimchi," Mrs. Han said after I fished the meat out. I tasted a small piece. Kimchi sure was a spicy veggie with a lot of "character." Dad always says that about hot foods.

"So your family's Italian?" Ok-hee asked.

"Seriously Italian. We eat pasta three times a week and we all talk with our hands." I took a big gulp of water. Sesame seeds were floating on top from the stray *bulgogi*.

"My best friend Lisa in Flushing is Italian. Her mom makes this delicious bean soup with tomatoes and macaroni," Ok-hee said.

"Pasta fagioli. My mom has a hundred-year-old family recipe, only she loads it up with sausage. I call it fagioli carnivory. Mmm, makes my mouth water."

"Ok-hee's a vegetarian," Yongsu whispered.

Mr. Han quickly turned the conversation to school. "So, Joseph, do you get good grades?" he asked, scooping more rice into his bowl.

"Straight As, most of the time."

Ok-hee rolled her eyes. "School matters more than happiness to Korean parents," she said.

"Working hard helps you *find* happiness," Mr. Han

141

quickly answered. His Adam's apple bobbed up and down as he spoke.

All this good-student talk made me nervous. *What if they asked about my essay?*

Redirect the conversation. Like Mom does when customers suggest dyeing their hair ridiculous colors. "What do you miss most about Korea, Mr. Han?"

He paused. "In Korea, young people show respect for elders. They understand that age has earned such respect. Not so here."

I nodded. Dad would agree with Mr. Han, though he'd say it in his own Jersey way.

"Would you like to visit Korea, Joseph?" he asked.

"Definitely. I want to check out Pusan." I tried to chew without opening my mouth.

"My brother and I worked at the Pusan docks in the summer when we were your age," he said.

I thought about the police station where they found me, wondering how far it was from those docks. Mr. Han could have passed that station every day when he was a kid.

"People from Pusan are different." Mr. Han smiled at Mrs. Han. "Wouldn't you agree?"

She nodded as she poured soy sauce over her rice. "They have a funny accent, like Americans down South.

And they are . . . how can I explain? Straight talkers, they speak their mind. You understand?"

"Sure," I said. Like me, I thought, suddenly getting excited. *She's describing me!*

"Pusan has beautiful sandy beaches," Mr. Han said. "And it's very hilly. If you arrive there at night, you think, Look at all the tall buildings lit up! But in daylight, you see they are hills with one-story houses, not skyscrapers."

I bit into another piece of *bulgogi*. My stomach was expanding like a water balloon. I wanted Mr. Han to describe Pusan's hills, the docks, the kids playing whatever games kids play there. Finally I'd be able to fill in the details of my déjà-vu dream. To know what it was like where I was born.

"Joseph won a school essay contest about his Korean family," Ok-hee announced.

"Didn't you write about Sohn Kee Chung?" Yongsu asked.

Every Han stopped chewing.

"What was your essay about?" Mr. Han asked, his eyes wide.

Gulp.

"Nothing special. Basic Korean stuff." My forehead was shooting sweat like a busted fire hydrant.

Somehow Yongsu and Ok-hee mustn't have heard about Essaygate. Time to redirect again. "So, what's your favorite part of Korea, Ok-hee?" I asked.

"Right now Ok-hee's favorite place is Europe," Yongsu said as he mixed kimchi in with his *bulgogi*. "She wants to study abroad."

"I've lived in Korea and America. I want to check out someplace else," Ok-hee said, pouting. "Mrs. Peroutka says we should think about global careers. You want me to be successful, don't you?"

"Remember, you are thirteen years old, not twenty," Mrs. Han answered. "More kimchi, Joseph?"

"Yes, please." I could feel bullets flying in this Han family cross fire. It was a familiar feeling, given my feisty twin sisters. "My parents can't agree on a favorite Italian city. Mom says Naples, but Dad says Florence. They're both loyal to where their parents were born."

Ok-hee smiled. "I'd love to spend a semester in Italy. And tenth grade would be perfect, before all that college entrance prep begins."

"What language do you study?" Mrs. Han asked me.

"Spanish." Didn't most kids take Spanish, except the ones whose parents force French on them?

"Ok-hee takes Italian," Mrs. Han said. "We do not understand why."

"Because it's a beautiful language. And if I study there, I'll use it," she answered. She sounded satisfied, like when Sophie has a good comeback for Mom.

Mr. and Mrs. Han just kept eating.

"Do you know anything about the Korean language?" Mr. Han asked.

I shook my head.

"Korean is considered a 'polite language' because the words spoken may be formal or informal, depending on the person you are addressing. It is based on Hangul, the Korean alphabet with twenty-four characters. Which is the—"

"Most perfect writing system in the world," Yongsu and Ok-hee said in unison, imitating their father.

"This is true," Mr. Han said, amused.

"We've been studying Hangul every Saturday since we left Korea, just in case we forget it." Yongsu groaned.

I smiled at him sympathetically, like what a pain that would be. But the truth was, I wished I could speak Korean too.

After dinner we carried our dishes to the kitchen. I handed Mrs. Han the empty *bulgogi* platter.

"Gamsa hamnida," I said, trying hard to make the right sounds.

She bowed and smiled back.

Yongsu and I stacked the dishes in the sink. Mrs. Han washed and Ok-hee dried. There was no dishwasher in sight.

"*Uhmma*, I need a haircut," Ok-hee said to her mother.

"Joseph's mother cuts hair very nice," Mrs. Han said.

"And you could practice your Italian on her," I added.

Ok-hee touched her barrette, the way girls always do when they're talking about hair.

Dad was reading in his recliner when I got home. "There's blueberry pie in the fridge," he called from behind *The Great Gatsby*.

"I'm stuffed." I walked past him toward the stairs.

He looked like he expected me to start a conversation. Why did it always have to be me? *He* could've asked how things went at the Hans.

I hadn't even reached the top step when Mom's questions began. "Tell me all about it," she said, walking out of the bathroom with a mud mask on her face.

"Apparently I fit the profile of a Pusaner perfectly," I said. I explained how the Hans described Pusaners as straight-talking, no-nonsense types.

Mom laughed. With the mud caked on her face, she looked like a sci-fi creature trapped in a bathrobe. "That sounds like you, all right. Did you enjoy the dinner?"

"Korean mothers make huge quantities of food, just like Italian moms," I said, patting my stomach. "And the *bulgogi* was awesome."

"I'm glad you liked it, honey. Next time I see Mrs. Han, I'll ask for her recipe. We Calderaros need to lay off the cream sauce anyway. So they treated you well?"

"I guess . . . ," I said with hesitation.

"What is it, Joseph?"

"They don't think I'm one of them. *Real* Korean. I can tell."

Mom looked at me, long and hard. "You've got 'real' written all over your beautiful face," she said, and she kissed my forehead before sending me off to bed.

A Message from St. Louis

Nash was standing at the bottom of my driveway when I headed for the bus stop the next morning. He hadn't walked to my house before school since we carried dinosaur backpacks and feared the bully with a water gun. Something was up.

"We got an e-mail back on your search," he said as the bus screeched in the distance. He looked like he was bursting to get this out, but serious, too.

My stomach fluttered. "What's it say?"

He pulled a paper from his backpack. "Here, read it."

Joseph,

My name is Jae Park Leonis and I might be able
to help you. I'm 27 years old and I grew up in
Pusan. I came here to St. Louis five years ago.
The date you were found brings back family
memories. I found myself scanning this website
for that very reason.

                                    Call me.

                                    Jae

I stared at the telephone number printed on the bottom
of the e-mail. Nash hovered next to me, anxious to hear
what I'd say.

"You think this guy Jae is for real? Maybe he's trying
to rope me into a sucker scam, like 'Buy this fail-proof
adoption search kit for only $49.95.'"

Nash shrugged his shoulders. "He sounds like he's
telling the truth."

The school bus pulled up and we got on.

"You gonna call him, Joseph?" Nash asked.

"I think so. I mean, what have I got to lose, right?"

"That's the spirit. Tell me what he says, okay?"

"Definitely."

"Joseph, what's the haps, Drummer Boy!" Frankie
called as I stepped on the bus.

"Hey dude," I answered, but I kept walking.

I would phone St. Louis after school today. After all, Jae could be my brother. I just might find something out before writing my revised essay. Talk about a drummer's lucky timing.

But then why did my palms feel so sweaty?

The world was suddenly spinning fast for a Friday morning. *Very* fast.

The rest of the day dragged like somebody stuffed an extra five hours in it. How could I concentrate on textbooks when I had a bombshell phone number in my pocket?

Finally I arrived home to a hushed house. Nobody but Frazer chewing away on a bone. Dad was working, Mom was at the shop with Gina, and Sophie had soccer. For the first time in ages, I skipped a snack. I even thought about skipping the phone call—too much pressure. But I silenced Chicken Calderaro. I needed to talk to Jae.

My hands were shaking as I pulled the paper from my pocket and dialed the phone number.

Right away someone answered, but it wasn't a guy.

"Yes, this is Jae. I'm happy to talk with you, Joseph." She had a soft voice and an Asian accent, though not as thick as Mrs. Han's.

In the background I heard a little kid's voice.

Jae asked how old I was, where I lived, what grade I was in, and even what my hobbies were. I felt like she was one of those mall walkers with a clipboard doing consumer research.

"So you think you might know about my, umm, my birth mother?" I finally blurted out.

She paused. "Maybe. You see, I grew up in—"

Suddenly I got an earful of long-distance crying.

"I'm sorry, Joseph. My son is upset. He needs something to eat. Can we talk another day?"

"Yeah, sure, I'll call you back," I said, speaking loud over the wails, but feeling low. After fourteen years of waiting, I got preempted by a kid with the munchies.

"Mine!"

"Uh-uh, mine!"

What a painful déjà vu. It was a bright warm day and I sat staring at the computer screen that was just as blank as my brain. Sophie and Gina were in the kitchen arguing about whose hiccups were louder. It sounded like they'd been inhaling helium.

"Finish your lunch," Dad snapped as their pup-squeaks grew more annoying. I could see he was tired of the Mr. Mom Saturday Routine. Finally Sophie and Gina jumped up from the table, ignoring their half-eaten sandwiches and apple slices, and ran outside to play.

I had three more days to finish Version Two of my essay and I still hadn't figured out what to write. I couldn't include what I'd learned from Jae because I hadn't learned a thing. I'd called her back twice and both times I got an answering message with her son singing "Puff the Magic Dragon."

Forget writer's block—I had writer's blockhead. How could I write about *anything* when I knew something big was about to reveal itself via St. Louis?

Yesterday I'd scribbled a half-page tribute to Nonno Calderaro. I mean, he was a gutsy guy. Dad told me that when Nonno arrived in Manhattan, a French immigrant pulled a knife on him and stole his wallet. He chased the thief in the heat for an hour until he caught him. But I couldn't fold it into a story that felt like mine. I kept getting hung up on the essay topic: "*Your* Heritage."

Next I tried to summarize the history of Korea. But I hadn't reached the thirteenth century before I got mixed up about who invaded who and what the Mongols had to do with Korea, anyway.

And in a last, lame attempt, I'd typed "A Tribute to a Gold Horn" on top of the page. But all I could think about was Dad's Mad Meter racing on my birthday, Mom's *mal-*

occhio musings, and Sophie starting a Save the Goats campaign. It was stand-up comedy material, but a dark kind of funny that I didn't want to share.

So far, the computer screen was still blank.

Dad was sitting at the kitchen table, drinking lemonade and eating leftovers. "Want some calamari, Joseph?" he called.

"Thanks, but I prefer my squid straight from the sea to the frying pan." Mom travels to Perth Amboy, New Jersey, just to get catch-of-the-day squid from the boats off the Raritan Bay, and you can tell. Her fried calamari is the perfect combination of gummy squid and light, crispy batter. But to me, seafood leftovers taste soggy. Mom says she's turned me into a spoiled calamari connoisseur at an early age.

"What are you working on, Joseph?" Dad called.

"My essay."

"Which one?"

"For social studies, the ancestry story." Was he that out of touch? This essay had only started World War III in our house.

"How's it coming?" he asked as he sprinkled red pepper on his food.

"I might as well be writing instructions for constructing an artificial kneecap."

He turned his chair to face me. "Why?"

"I don't know what to write."

"How about your visit with the Hans? Mom said they shared a lot with you."

I wanted to give Dad the silent treatment, because he hadn't been interested in my visit earlier. But then I glanced at him, and I saw this fragile look in his eye, like the beluga whales at Sea World.

So I told him that I used chopsticks at the Hans' house, and that the food was awesome.

"Kimchi is even hotter than Mom's jalapeño poppers," I said. Dad and I are the only ones in the family who can stomach those. They go down your throat like mini-fireballs, but they're delicious.

I even told Dad what Mr. Han said about people from Pusan.

"They're straight shooters, huh? You sure fit that description," he said, laughing. "So why aren't you writing? Sounds like you've got some material to work with."

I looked outside. Sophie and Gina were seated on the glider swing, squealing as they soared higher and higher. One minute my sisters were ready to kill each other, and the next they were giddy. Kind of like Dad and me.

"Know what, Dad? I think I'm an ethnic sandwich.

One hunk of Joseph slapped between a slice of Italian bread and a mound of Korean sticky rice."

He walked over and put his hand on my shoulder.

"Maybe that's not such a bad combination."

"That's 'cause it's not you," I said, staring down at the floor.

"I'm not you, Joseph, and I can't imagine how it feels to be adopted. But I know how it feels to wonder if I'm doing what I was meant to do. I ask myself that almost every night as I rinse out my sponges and load my ladders back on the truck. And I'm no psychologist, but I know you're a fine kid. The best you could be—Italian *and* Korean. Maybe that's the angle you oughtta take for your essay."

"Maybe shmaybe," I replied.

Dad still didn't understand. But he *had* given me something to write about.

I turned in that blasted essay at the end of class on Tuesday. I'd stayed up past midnight finishing it, and I couldn't wait to hand it to Mrs. Peroutka.

"Joseph, the Ethnic Sandwich." A fifteen-hundred-word ancestry tale that read like a buffet. A little about Buddha Baby's American debut, or how I arrived at JFK Airport from Korea. A little about my grandparents' tailor shop. A bit about Dad's boxing past. And some on those straight-talkers from Pusan. Finally, I threw in a mini-lesson on Italian superstitions and the *malocchio*.

I knew this version wouldn't win a contest, but this time it was the God Honest Truth from a former Cub Scout: how it felt to be Joseph Calderaro—Korean on the outside, Italian on the inside, and sometimes the other way around.

And I wouldn't say this around my parents or Mrs. Peroutka, but I felt proud of "Joseph, the Ethnic Sandwich."

It was *my* story.

Shrimp Connection

Ahh, the sounds of silence.

I came home from school a few days later and was glad the only mouth nearby was connected to Frazer's snout—and he was snoring. I'd spent the whole lunch period listening to Frankie's verbal delusions about which top-tier girl he was asking to the Farewell Formal. I couldn't stand hearing any more. It reminded me of how my year-long plan to ask Kelly had gone up in flames.

The empty house gave me a chance to concentrate on the phone call I had to make to Jae. I poured a glass of iced tea and dialed Jae's number.

"Is this a good time to talk?" I asked.

"Yes, Kevin is sleeping. And I'm taking a break after a busy day of auditing."

Jae had her own accounting firm and worked from home. I told her Mom and Dad both owned businesses. Jae especially liked hearing that Mom owned a hair salon. I could just imagine the two of them talking about what hairstyles were hot here and in the Midwest. Jae said she'd never visited New Jersey, though she knew the "Which exit?" joke.

"I've never been to Saint Louis," I told her.

She and Kevin liked to visit the Missouri Botanical Garden. "We feed these giant Japanese koi fish there. Every time Kevin spots one, he splashes and screams with joy. I think the fish want to scream when they see him, too."

I laughed. It felt like I had known Jae forever. She was so easy to talk to.

"About Kevin," I said, "his name doesn't sound too Korean."

"You're right. My husband, Scott, is from Independence, Missouri."

That surprised me. I'd expected Jae to be like Mrs. Han, 100 percent Korean, even in her choice of a husband.

I told Jae about my dinner at the Hans. She giggled when I called myself the Master Chopstick Impersonator. But she interrupted when I said the Hans were the first real Koreans I'd ever met.

"What do you mean *real*?"

"Authentic, not adopted," I explained.

"So that makes someone a real Korean and you *not* real?"

"Yeah, being adopted Korean is different. It's sort of like wearing one of those fake stones they sell on TV—a cubic zirconium—and passing it off as a diamond."

"I suggest you consider yourself a diamond, only cut differently," Jae said.

I looked up at the kitchen clock as we spoke. Almost dinnertime. A hungry Calderaro might burst through the door any minute. So like a true Pusaner, I cut to the chase. "Do you know anything about me, Jae?"

"It's possible," she answered cautiously.

She explained that her Aunt Hea had a baby fourteen years ago. A baby, she said, that nobody talked about and nobody ever saw. "My uncle left my aunt and my three little cousins. He had a drinking problem, and he'd lost his job. Shortly after he moved out, I remember that my aunt looked fatter in the belly. But it's the Korean way not to talk much about these things."

Half of my brain concentrated on what Jae was saying; the other half raced wildly.

Jae could be my cousin. I could have sisters and brothers in Pusan. My mother's name could be Hea!

"The day you were found, May seventh . . . I remember it because in Korea, it's close to Children's Day, May fifth. My parents were having a party, and my aunt brought my cousins. Her face looked sunken, and she didn't have a big belly anymore. She didn't have a baby, either."

"What did your aunt do with her baby?" My heart pounded louder than a bass drum. Louder than six bass drums. I was ready to fit the final piece into the MBA puzzle.

"I asked my mother once, and she changed the subject. My aunt took a job waitressing at a coffee shop. Nobody ever talked about the baby, and I knew I wasn't supposed to either."

"Mommy! Mommy!" Kevin's squeaky voice called, and she whispered back to him in Korean.

I tried to remember what I knew: my birth mother named me Duk-kee. I was left outside the Pusan police station in a basket, with a blanket and a note. An old lady found me in the afternoon after returning from the market.

"Jae, is anyone in your family named Duk-kee?"

"That's my uncle's name. My mom and Aunt Hea's older brother. Why do you ask?"

"My birth mother named me Duk-Kee. Where did your aunt live in Pusan?"

Jae said her family lived in the same row of small houses as Aunt Hea's, up on a hill, not far from the docks. I knew all about those docks and hills.

"My father worked on the boats. My mother used to take us to the market nearby. Before he left, my uncle sold fish from a cart. Sometimes he'd give us big, plump shrimp that my mother would steam for dinner."

That could've been the market that the old lady was walking from when she found me. The market where my real father sold shrimp. No wonder I love shrimp!

"Does your aunt still live in Pusan?" I asked.

"Yes. She's remarried now, actually, to the owner of the coffee shop. One of her sons, my cousin Chulsu, graduated from university and came to America like me. He's a computer programmer for Microsoft."

My real brother could be hacking away at a computer, side by side with Bill Gates!

"What's your aunt's last name?" I asked. I was seconds away from identifying this phantom lady who's loomed over me my whole life. I'd say her full name out loud and—*presto!* She'd be real.

161

I didn't hear an answer. Mom, Sophie, Gina, and Aunt Foxy burst through the door, talking and laughing all at once.

"Sorry, Jae. I've got to go." I hung up quickly. I'd just uncovered the most incredible news of my life, but I couldn't imagine sharing it with anybody yet. Especially my family.

"Hiya, Joseph!" Aunt Foxy called out.

"Hi," I said, trying to act normal, even if my hands were trembling.

"What, you're too big to kiss your godmother?" She wrapped her arms tight around me. I could smell Shear Impressions's body-fragrance-of-the-month on her clothes.

"I better get my hugs now before those high school girls notice your good looks and stylish haircuts," she said.

Sophie started searching through the snack cupboard, ignoring Mom's threats about not eating before dinner. Meanwhile Gina unloaded her backpack, spilling a bag of pretzels on the floor. But before anyone could say "Back off, boxer," Frazer had gobbled them up.

"Aunt Foxy's staying for supper," Gina told me with her eyes aglow.

"But the bad news is Mommy's making meatball heroes." Sophie pouted. "Ground guts, yuck! I'm having a special veggie burger. *And* I get to sit next to Aunt Foxy."

"No fair!" Gina cried.

Mom ignored Sophie and Gina. She was listening to Aunt Foxy rave about her new boyfriend, who was a producer for the cable company.

"I'm telling you, Maria, he's different from the other clowns I've dated. Dominick's a perfect gentleman—and sweet, too. Remember when I was sick last week? He brought me orange juice and chicken noodle soup."

"Just for you? Or does he make deliveries for every attractive woman he sees blowing her nose?" Mom grinned.

"C'mon, you haven't even met him," Aunt Foxy said, laughing. She turned to me. "What do you think, Joseph? Dominick's a diehard Yankees fan with season tickets."

"He can't be a total jerk if he roots for the Yankees," I said. Wanting to avoid more talk, I brushed past her on my way upstairs.

Aunt Foxy gave me a curious look, as if she wondered why I wasn't goofing around with her like usual. But I just couldn't. My brain was overloaded. I needed to lie down and rewind everything I'd just heard from Jae.

• • •

In my dream that night, I was back on that dirt road in Korea. My clothes were sweaty as I trekked up a hill, and my arm hurt from pulling the wagon. I must have fallen behind, because all my companions were ahead of me.

My breath was heavy and I wanted to stop and rest, but then I saw her at the top of the hill. My birth mother. She was short and stocky like me and wearing a red dress. Everything about her was crystal clear except for her face. As usual, that was out of focus, even as I got closer.

She recognized me right away.

"Duk-kee," she shouted, waving wildly. "I've been waiting. Hurry!"

The wagon bumped up and down as I charged toward her. Huffing and puffing, I ran until I could almost reach out and touch her, when suddenly I heard:

"Your friendly neighborhood wall crawler says rise and shine!"

My Spider-Man alarm woke me, and I realized I had never heard her voice. I had never, ever seen my birth mother at all. I was crushed.

But she was out there. And I got to thinking, like Dad always says, "The ball's in my court." I needed to make this happen.

Jae and I had found each other, against the odds. I knew that she *had* to be my cousin. This was no time for Chicken Calderaro to appear. I had to overcome the obstacles—to keep going until I got the answers I needed.

A Man with a Plan

I'd come home from school the next day expecting a quiet house again. I needed to call Jae, to ask her if she would speak with her aunt. But instead I found Dad stretched out on the patio chaise longue with Mom beside him, rubbing his shoulder.

"Geez, Dad, what happened?"

"On-the-job casualty, son. Humpty Dumpty does windows," he said, his eyes darting to the cast on his arm. He had a bandage above his eye and a few scrapes on his cheek.

"It was only a matter of time, Vinny," Mom said, taking

an empty glass from Dad. "What were you thinking, climbing a three-story Victorian to wash old windows stuck shut for twenty years?"

"I'm sorry, Dad. Does it hurt?" I asked.

"Not too much. I just added a few more scars to my weathered look. How can I grumble? I've got the best nurse this side of the Garden State Parkway. And she's cute to look at," Dad said, pointing at Mom.

Mom smiled but looked concerned. "You're getting out of that business, you hear me? You deserve better. Look at the books you read!"

She went into the kitchen to refill Dad's lemonade. I sat on the picnic bench. For a few minutes we said nothing. Both our eyes wandered to the magazine resting on the side table, *The New Yorker*.

"How long are you going to be out of work?"

"A couple of weeks," he replied.

Calderaro Window Washers is a one-man operation. As Dad says, all the profits and all the headaches come from one squeegee cleaner. I looked at his broken arm and knew this was going to be rough for business.

"I can help out, especially with school almost over. I'm bigger than I was last summer when I worked for you. And this time I won't leave streaks. Promise."

Dad smiled. A happy smile, not like you'd expect from a

guy who'd just fallen off a ladder, broken his arm, and messed up his business. "No, Joseph. You focus on your schoolwork until the very last day. I'll adapt. Believe it or not, I think this accident was the best thing in the world that could have happened to me."

Frazer trotted over and plunked down between us.

"Yup, the best thing in the world," Dad said again.

"I give up. Why?"

"Because I got a wake-up call. One minute I was climbing a ladder, on my way to the top of some divorce attorney's million-dollar mansion. I probably would've cleared a nice chunk of change for an afternoon's work, and you know how I felt?"

I wanted to say, "Off balance?" but I shook my head instead.

"Miserable. Unfulfilled. The next thing I know, I lose my grip and fall into a juniper bush. Broke the same arm I broke boxing twenty years ago. So I drove myself with one hand to the ER and in my head I heard this voice saying, 'Vincenzo, this could be the sign you've been waiting for. Get out of the window-washing business. Today it's a broken arm. Who knows? Tomorrow it could be a broken soul.'"

The part about falling off a ladder as a sign was more typical of Mom than Dad, but I kept my wisecracks to myself. For once, Dad was pouring his heart out.

"So you're going to sell the business?"

"I'm not going to do anything dumb. We still have a mortgage. But in the meantime, I'm going to visit the local college and figure out how to get my degree. Night classes, weekends, whatever. I'll do it. I've always wanted to teach."

Dad uses every opportunity he can to talk about books and how they relate to life. "I can see you stomping around the campus," I said, grinning.

"Why not—and why not now, huh? I'm not getting any younger, but I'm not ready for the senior citizen special at the diner either."

"Just on the basketball court," I said. I couldn't resist.

"I'll play you one on one, even with a bad wing. Seriously, it's time to chase my dream, to stop with the shoulda, coulda, woulda's. I want to bring great books to a generation of video game addicts. What do you think?"

I pictured my father helping students understand what Edgar Allan Poe meant when he freaked out over that raven. Dad has a wacky way of tossing words together like vegetables in stew, but he knows what he's talking about. And he sure loves books.

"It sounds like you're a man with a plan, Dad."

Mom returned to the patio, bringing Dad more lemonade.

"Come here, Maria," he said, and kissed her on the lips. "You're looking at a man with a plan."

I caught a ride to band with Nash on Monday morning. We were late because Nash's mom had trouble getting her prehistoric van started—so late that they'd already started "Jamaican Farewell" when I opened the squeaky band-room door. Yongsu gave me a sympathetic look from the flute section. I expected Mrs. Athena to point her conductor's wand disapprovingly like she does when kids dash in mid-song, but she didn't. I think she knows I hate being late.

Robyn caught up with me after practice as I put my drumsticks away and gathered my books. "Hey, Joseph. You hear about the Buddhist who refused to take Novocain at the dentist?"

I was too sleepy to figure this one out.

"He wanted to transcend dental medication," she said, grinning.

"Good one." I smiled, and a yawn popped out.

"What're you, a vampire?" she asked. "You've got black circles under your eyes."

"I haven't been getting much sleep lately. A lot on my mind."

"Something happen?"

"What hasn't happened? For one, my dad had an accident."

Robyn stopped in the middle of the hallway. "Even *you* wouldn't make that up. Is he okay?"

"He broke his arm. My dad's the Rocky Balboa of Nutley, New Jersey. He's actually happier now," I said, shaking my head. "Parents."

"Rough time lately, huh? First kids spread rumors about you, and now your dad gets hurt."

"It's not that bad. I could've gotten E. coli bacteria from the cafeteria or chopped off a finger in Life Skills." I waved my hands with my thumbs tucked in.

Robyn didn't come back with a joke. "Only losers pay attention to the rumor of the day. I didn't believe any of that stuff about the essay contest. I kept telling everyone to stick it down their esophaguses."

We climbed the main stairwell. All the way up I felt bad about Robyn defending me and my not coming clean.

"Listen, Robyn. I *did* make up the essay about my Korean grandfather. The guy really won a gold medal, but we weren't related. That's why my essay got canned."

I looked down at a dirt spot on my sneaker, feeling stained inside, too.

Robyn tugged at my T-shirt sleeve. "Did you make that up because you're adopted?"

"Yeah, kind of. It's a long story," I said, looking up at her. For the first time I noticed her eyes. They were greenish-brown and swirly, like lake water in the fall.

"That sucks worse than an industrial vacuum. People not understanding, I mean." She shook her head.

At her locker Robyn started telling me about her cousin's husband's sister's kid, or something like that, who was ten and had leukemia.

"You know what's worse than having a disease that might kill you and makes you bald at ten?"

"What?"

"Having jerks ask if you're going to die. Jesse told me he was tired of all the questions and the staring in school. Well, naturally I armed him with sharp comebacks."

"Like what?"

"I told him to poke 'em between their dumb bunny eyes and ask them what disease caused them to be mentally defective—and ugly!"

I laughed. "You're vicious!"

"No, I just look out for the people who matter," she said.

In study hall that afternoon, Robyn and I shared the marble pound cake we'd made in Life Skills. I was confused about quadratic equations, and we sat there sneaking cake while she explained the FOIL technique for solving them. In a *niente per niente* return favor, I let her borrow my Great Depression notes, since she'd been sleeping during the second half of social studies.

As Robyn copied my notes, I noticed Kelly across the room, talking with her friends. I take that back—her friends were *listening*. Kelly's lips were moving ninety miles per hour. For a second our eyes locked, but then she looked away, disgusted, like she'd spotted roadkill.

Why had I ever fallen for her? As Gina would say, "She is *not* nice."

"Joseph, your worksheet fell," Robyn said, picking up a piece of paper off the floor.

"Thanks." I studied Robyn's hands when she gave it to me. She had perfectly shaped, half-moon fingernails. She wore a silver ring on her pinkie with a dangling peace sign. She was cute, I realized. Funny, I've never thought of crazy Robyn that way.

"What is it, Joseph?" Robyn asked. "Your eyes are glazed over like you've been hypnotized."

I snapped out of it. "Nothing. I mean, you look very, um, put together today."

"And I really like your elbows," she replied in a deep, throaty voice. "They're so . . . *bendable*."

I couldn't help laughing.

As I left study hall, I thought again about going to the Farewell Formal. Only this time it wasn't Kelly's hand I imagined I was holding.

Detour on Discovery Road

"If it's *not* strep throat, it's definitely a tumor on my tonsils," I groaned. I was slumped in Dad's recliner, wearing an undershirt and boxers.

Mom pressed her hand against my forehead. "You're not even hot," she snapped in an unsympathetic voice.

"Don't you think I'm a little old for schoolitis? Nobody fakes it in June, Mom."

Finally she gave in. She didn't sound the official "Stay home from school" decree, but she did say there was plenty of juice in the fridge.

"I've got a customer waiting for a cap highlight. I'll

call you later!" she yelled as she clomp-clomped out the door in her platform sandals.

Victory.

My throat *did* feel a bit scratchy. But more importantly, I had a phone call to make. Dad was visiting college Admissions, but he'd be back by the time school ended, so I wouldn't have had a chance to talk privately with Jae. "Do, or do not. There is no try." That's what Yoda tells Luke in *The Empire Strikes Back*, and that wrinkly little alien was wise. If I wanted to connect with my birth mother, it was up to me to do it.

Right away I dialed Jae. She sounded happy to hear from me. And thankfully she didn't ask why I wasn't in school. She shared a funny story about how Kevin dressed up as a superhero, and naturally I approved. Then I found myself spewing out news about Dad's accident and how it somehow led him to apply to college. I even told Jae how badly I wanted to take Robyn to the Farewell Formal.

"Ask her, Joseph," she said in a big-sister voice. "Be polite and sincere—like a gentleman—and I bet she'll accept."

"I doubt Robyn would use 'gentleman' to describe me, but my best friend Nash says I have a way of charming parents. It's my Italian upbringing."

Jae laughed.

What was I thinking with all this chitchat? My phone time was limited. I had to cut to the chase.

I cleared my throat. "Jae, I've been thinking about writing to your Aunt Hea," I said, my voice cracking a little. "Introducing myself and sending my picture. Will you give me her address?"

A pause.

"Do your parents know we've talked?" she asked.

"Um, not yet."

I heard a door slam on Jae's end.

"Joseph, we're not sure yet that you're my aunt's child. I think we should do some checking before we talk to her."

Suddenly Jae seemed like another detour on the road to discovery.

"My parents don't know any more about me than I've already told you, and this isn't exactly their favorite subject," I explained.

"Would they let you talk with the adoption agency? They must know something more than we do. I wouldn't dare speak to my aunt unless we were absolutely certain. I just couldn't."

"What, the thought of being related to me would put her in shock?" I was only half kidding.

"I know this is exciting for you, Joseph, but it could be difficult for my aunt. We have to be sensitive."

I didn't want to hear that. I wanted Jae to say Aunt Hea would be high-fiving everyone in Pusan after she got my letter. That she'd frame my eighth-grade photo and put it on her dresser. Maybe she'd even hop on the next Korean Air flight direct to JFK to meet me.

"If I talk to my parents and the agency, will you tell your aunt about me?" I asked.

Kevin was chanting in the background. "Juice! Juice! Juice!"

"You're almost as persistent as Kevin. Yes, talk to your parents and the adoption agency. And if the facts check out, I'll call Aunt Hea."

I was the only one in my family available to play cheerleader at Sophie's soccer game Saturday morning. Mom was working, Gina had started her singing class at the Y, and Dad had another appointment at the college.

This was Sophie's last game before the playoffs, and her team was undefeated. You'd think eight-year-olds would be only moderately intense about a sport, right? It's not like they're squaring off for the World Cup or anything. Well, think again, because Sophie was on the elite travel team. These girls meant kick-butt business, with scabs on their elbows and bruises on their knees to prove it. But tough as she is, Sophie gets upset if we're not there to cheer her on. So, marshmallow-hearted brother that I am, I rode my bike three miles to the soccer fields, along with Nash. I'd invited Yongsu, too, but he had to go to Korean school. Yongsu frowned when he told me that, but I said Korean school sounded awesome.

Of course, Mom had bribed me with some moolah if I watched the game, but that was beside the point.

The wind blasted more like March than June, and the bike ride was all uphill. Sophie's team had already scored the first goal by the time we got there. She was playing midfield, one on one against a girl built like a mobile home. But Sophie didn't seem fazed. With gritted teeth and a messy ponytail, she kicked the ball right around the girl like she was running to save civilization.

Nash and I stood by the sideline. Sophie's friend Kaylie was alone guarding the goal. She waved to me.

"Coach finally put me in for goalie, Joseph. My first time!" she shouted.

I cupped my hands to my mouth. "Don't let the other team hear that!"

After we sat on the bleachers, Nash asked me about Jae.

"The whole search is stuck in the mud. Jae won't tell

her aunt about me until I talk to my parents, and that's a waste of time."

"Maybe they'll surprise you once they see how strong you feel about this."

"I've had enough surprises lately," I said.

A curly-haired kid from the other team broke away with the ball. In a desperate ditch effort, Sophie slide tackled her.

Toot. The referee's whistle. "Yellow card on Ten."

"Out, Sophie!" her coach shouted, and she stomped off the field.

After Sophie returned to the game, a tall girl stole the ball from her and made a breakaway downfield. Kaylie leaped for the ball, jumping-jack style, but it swerved past her shoulder into the goal.

The crowd cheered. Sophie pounded her leg with her fist.

I thought about what Nash had said. Maybe Mom and Dad *would* be more open to helping me search. After all, Dad seemed to be on a high since the accident, as weird as that sounded. And I remembered what Mom told me when she found out about my fake essay. She said she wished I'd talked to her first; she would've wanted to help.

At the very least they might speak to the adoption

agency for me. Privacy laws probably wouldn't allow me to find out anything more about how I was found without Mom and Dad being involved anyway.

The wind picked up again during the second half. Nash and I moved to the far end of the bleachers, where the breeze was at our back. We had parked ourselves on the bottom row when a bunch of girls from school arrived. I recognized a few of them from Kelly's crowd.

They glanced at us with less-than-enthused expressions.

"No wonder none of them won Most Friendly for the yearbook," I told Nash.

"So who are you asking to the Farewell Formal?" Nash asked.

"You tell first."

"I want to ask Ok-hee, but I doubt she'd go with me."

"Why not? Besides being obsessed with Wolverine, you're practically normal."

"Ha-ha. Spoken by a guy who looks up to a web spinner. But seriously, Ok-hee acts mature, like a high schooler. And she's *really* smart. She composes music and reads the same books as your dad."

"Ever heard of multiple intelligence? You're smart too, in different ways. You work that computer almost as well as you play trumpet. Ok-hee might seem sophisticated, but trust me. Her world is full of lip gloss and mall madness. I even saw her reading *Teen People* once."

Nash laughed. "What's that got to do with anything?"

"It means she's reachable. All you've got to do is come up with a catchy way to grab her attention."

"Like what, interrupting morning announcements and asking her out over the PA system?"

I shook my head. "She'd never speak to you again if you pulled that one."

I didn't have an answer, but I could tell that Nash felt encouraged. *Think,* Joseph. What did I remember about Ok-hee Han that could give us an idea? She wants to study abroad. She's a vegetarian. She takes Italian. . . .

She takes Italian!

A genius idea ricocheted inside my brain, like the soccer ball passing from one player to the next—though unfortunately those players were on the other team and running back again toward Kaylie.

I had a plan for Nash!

"Ok-hee takes Italian and loves all that European stuff. Write her a note in Italian and stick it in her locker. I bet she'll say yes faster than you can sing 'That's Amore.'"

Nash shook his head. "Forgettaboutit. I don't speak Italian."

But I knew who could. "Vinny Calderaro *lives* for this kind of stuff, Nash. You gush on paper, tell me what you want to say, and I'll ask my dad to write it *en Italiano*."

Nash shook my hand. "Deal—but only if you ask someone. You haven't told me who yet."

I shrugged. "I kinda like Robyn."

He nodded. "You two are always joking around in band."

"That's the problem. Robyn thinks I'm funnier than a beer commercial. But that's all I am. *Funny*."

"Funny is very in—with the right girl, that is," Nash said, glancing toward the snooty girls, then back at me. "Maybe someone should put in a good word for you."

I started to speak just as the other team scored again, seconds before the game clock ran out. Sophie's team was no longer undefeated.

After the players all shook hands, Sophie grabbed her water bottle and walked over to us. Laces were dragging from her cleats, her shin guard was twisted backward, and her elbow was cut.

I tugged on her ponytail. "You win some, you lose some."

She kicked the ground, sending a rock flying. "That referee didn't like me."

"No blaming, just shake it off," I said, sounding like Dad.

"*I'm* the reason we lost. I played crummy in the wind. Are you happy now?"

I looked at my sister. She was seconds away from a full-throttle meltdown.

"Forget it, Sophie. You've got the playoffs to save the good stuff for," Nash said.

Neither of us could get Sophie out of her funk. Tears poured down her dirt-streaked face. But then I remembered who could help Sophie recover: Andrew Jackson. He was crammed in my pocket on the twenty-dollar bill Mom gave me. "Sophie Teresa Calderaro, put on my helmet and hop on the back of my bike right now. I'm treating you and Nash to ice-cream sundaes, drowned in hot fudge and whipped cream. Who's afraid of lactose intolerance?"

That would've snapped Gina out of it, but Sophie sulked a little longer.

"I can't have any ice cream," Nash said.

"Huh?"

"I'm tracking what I eat and drink, remember? To see

what triggers my headaches. Right now I'm off dairy."

"How about candy?"

Nash nodded. "Candy works."

"Okay, a king-size whatever chocolate bar you want—on me."

Nash grinned. He looked pretty happy for a guy who couldn't eat ice cream.

"Time's up, Sophie. Either you come for ice cream or I drop you off at Mom's shop. And you know she'll make you sweep up hair."

Sophie looked up slyly. "Can I have an ice-cream float instead of a sundae?" she asked.

The ouch of her defeat was already subsiding.

An Elephant off My Back

S aturday night turned out to be a pizza-and-movie date at my house for me, Frazer, and two beautiful young women. Unfortunately, they were my sisters snuggling on the couch in matching Little Mermaid pajamas. Earlier Dad had returned from the college, swinging his cast merrily and talking nonstop about an American literature major. Mom decided this called for a night out, and arranged a double date with Aunt Foxy and her boyfriend.

I agreed to babysit for my sisters without a protest. I figured if Mom and Dad returned home from a rockin' good time, our talk might go better.

So Gina and Sophie and I watched *The Return of the Jedi*, my favorite of the Star Wars movies. We watched part of it, anyway. Gina fell asleep after ten minutes. Sophie hung in longer, but by the time Jabba the Hutt's sail barge blew up, she was snoring too. After I had carried them upstairs, one at a time, Mom and Dad's key turned in the door.

"What a love story." Mom flung her purse in the closet and kicked off her spiky heels. "I swear if I weren't hitched to your father, I'd track down that blond hottie, whatshisname."

Mom and Dad went into the family room. I heard them talking about Aunt Foxy.

"Did you notice how Dominick helped Foxy put her shawl on? That's a good sign. Seeing Foxy with a decent guy helps me sleep at night," Mom said.

Dad was already stretched out on the couch, buried behind the newspaper. Mom was snuggled beside him.

"I need to talk," I blurted out, looking from Mom to Dad. They raised their eyebrows nervously, like they were afraid that I'd messed up in school again.

Dad got up from the couch. "Let's go in the living room." He put his hand on Mom's back and led us there.

The last time we spoke in the living room was when

Dad gave me the "what-makes-boys-boys" spiel. He must have known this was serious.

I took a deep breath and told them everything. Dad's arms were folded over his chest; Mom's knees were crossed.

"I think Hea is my birth mother. Jae does too, but she says we should check this out with the adoption agency—just to be sure. Then she'll talk with her aunt. So . . . I need your help."

Dad swallowed. Mom kept nodding her head.

I shut my mouth and waited.

Mom spoke first. "Of course we'll help. We know how much this means to you, Joseph. Right, honey?" She squeezed Dad's hand.

Silence. The tick-tock of the hallway clock gave me something to concentrate on.

Finally Dad opened his mouth. "Have you thought this through, Joseph? About the search, what it means?"

I nodded.

"I understand being curious about your birth mother and where you come from, that's natural. I just think it's too soon to be doing this. You're only fourteen."

"Fourteen isn't four, Dad. I found this out all by myself so far."

"He can handle it, Vinny. Joseph needs to do this."

Mom was like a human bridge trying to connect Dad and me. But Dad kept shaking his head—not angry, because the Mad Meter wasn't running, but not ready to join my search party either. Yet I could tell he was trying, in his Dadish way, to understand.

"It's like you starting college, Dad, after all these years. You said you made decent money with the business, right? But that wasn't enough. There was more to you than just washing windows. Well, it's the same with me."

Dad rubbed his fingers slowly over the top of his cast. Then his eyes met mine, and I knew: he'd help.

"Maybe we can call the adoption agency on Monday," he said softly.

I felt relieved, like someone had taken an elephant off my back.

Mom's eye shadow sparkled and her whole face lit up. "I'm off on Monday. I'll call." Sure, she'd do the legwork, but this was the most involved Dad had ever been.

I told them how Jae said her aunt gave birth close to my birthday, right there in Pusan, and how the baby disappeared and was never mentioned again. And I wrote down Jae's phone number for Mom, in case the adoption agency needed to contact her directly.

"Guess what? Hea has a brother with my Korean

name, Duk-kee. I was probably named after him."

"Or maybe there are thousands of Duk-kee's running around Pusan," Dad added, "like all the Giovannis in Sicily."

Mom frowned at him. "Will you please try to be positive?"

"She's my birth mother. I know it," I said, purposely not looking at Mom. I just couldn't.

"Are they Christian, Joseph?" she asked. "Remember how I told you that the note from your birth mother asked that you be placed with a Christian family?"

"I think so." Actually, I'd forgotten to ask Jae that. But a gut feeling told me this would match up too, just like everything else Jae had said. Like the stars and planets on Mom's astrology charts when things were meant to be.

The clock chimed. Midnight. Mom yawned. We got up and headed upstairs.

"Joseph?" Dad called when I reached the top step.

"Yeah, Dad?"

"Doesn't matter if they're Korean, Italian, or Swahili—families are never perfect. Whatever you find, it's okay. You're my boy." He looked choked up.

"Don't worry," I said, and inside I felt happy that Dad was thinking about me that way. And that my parents and I were finally in this together.

"Go to bed, Mr. Tough Guy," Dad said, and he took Mom's hand as they walked toward their room.

I woke Monday morning even before Spider-Man zapped me with his danger alarm. My head felt like a two-lane highway with thoughts whizzing in opposite directions: first on contacting Hea after Mom spoke with the agency, and second on making plans for the Farewell Formal. Time was running out. I had to bite the bullet and ask Robyn. And I'd promised Nash that I'd get Dad to write the note for Ok-hee.

I laughed out loud as I ran downstairs. Nash and I were both hot on the trail of Korean women.

Dad was already in the kitchen, ready for work, when I walked in and stuck a Pop-Tart in the toaster. He'd hired a college student to help with business until he got the cast off, even though he said he'd still be working in a "limited way." How he'd limit himself as a window washer, I don't know, but he promised Mom he'd be careful.

He poured coffee into his Yankees mug. "You're up early, son."

"Today's a big day."

Dad nodded and sat down in front of his breakfast.

I grabbed my Pop-Tart from the toaster, and a pen

and pad from the kitchen drawer and sat next to him.

"Would you translate a letter into Italian, Dad?" Sometimes Nonno Calderaro still talked to Dad in Italian, especially when he was excited, so I knew he could.

"My spelling isn't so hot, but I could try. What's it for?"

"Nash wants to ask a girl to the Farewell Formal. We think writing a note in Italian might get her to say yes."

Dad reached for the pen and pad. "Good thing I didn't break my right arm. Go ahead, I'm ready for dictation, Caruso."

"Who's Caruso?" I bit into my Pop-Tart. Ouch, the filling burned my tongue.

"Only the greatest Italian tenor of all time. He was born in Naples. Talk about someone who had a way with the ladies."

I unfolded Nash's scribbled note and read it out loud:

Ok-hee,
You're smart and pretty. And you play piano like a pro. You also make me smile. Would you go to the Farewell Formal with me?
From your loyal lab partner,
Pete Nash

"Ok-hee doesn't sound like an Italian name," Dad said between bites of his bagel.

"It's Ok-hee Han. The Hans who bought the Jiffy Wash, remember?"

"The Korean family—where you had dinner?"

I nodded.

"This could only happen in New Jersey."

I felt goofy, sitting in the kitchen reading Nash's words to Dad, but I could tell he enjoyed playing Italian translator. Besides, what other choice did I have? Asking Mom to write the note would've been even more embarrassing, because then all the ladies in the shop would hear about it. And the only Italian my sisters knew were the swear words Mom yells when we're in trouble.

Dad scribbled it all down and slid the notepad over to me. "Tell Pete he's got the heart and soul of a romantic. Now who are you asking?"

"Robyn Carleton. She plays flute. And no, she doesn't read Italian."

He stood up and brought his dishes to the sink. "A girl with the gift of music. I like her already. Do you have any tricks up your sleeve to get her to say yes?"

"Nope. I'm just going to ask her. Straight up."

"Attaboy, Joseph," Dad said, picking up his keys. "Well, I better get going. We've got an apartment complex scheduled in Passaic today with lots of windows."

Then he paused. "Mom's going to call the agency for you later. Hopefully we'll get some answers."

He put on his Calderaro Window Washers cap and headed for the door. "Good luck today, Joseph."

"Thanks," I said. "You take it easy." But I couldn't help wondering—did he mean good luck with the adoption agency, or with Robyn?

Like When Billybob Died

The air felt soupy as I ran up the driveway after school that afternoon. Gina and Sophie were running through the sprinkler on the front lawn. Frazer lay on the soggy grass nearby with his tongue hanging out.

Nash had stayed after school, so I didn't know whether he'd given Ok-hee the note. And I hadn't seen Robyn all day, so I didn't get to ask her to the dance. But Mom always comes through when she makes a promise, and I was bursting to hear what the agency told her.

"Mommy's been on the phone talking about you," Gina shouted. The sprinkler gushed water into her face as she spoke.

I blew past her excitedly, my backpack banging up and down.

"What did they say?" I called as I charged into the kitchen.

Mom's face was flushed. She didn't answer, but she crossed her arms across her tank top and looked down at the kitchen floor.

"Did you call the agency?" I asked.

"Have some lemonade before we talk," she said.

Years ago, before we got Frazer, I had a pet hamster named Billybob. One day while I was at school, Mom found Billybob balled up stiff in the corner of the cage. That moment Mom had the same expression as when Billybob died.

"Tell me." I wiped my forehead.

Mom sat in a kitchen chair, but I kept standing, leaning against the fridge and tapping my foot. And not like I was playing the timpani for fun either.

"I'm sorry, Joseph. Hea can't be your birth mother. I called Jae today, before I called the adoption agency. To check on her aunt's religion. It turns out Hea isn't

Christian like your birth mother."

I swallowed hard. "So what? The agency could've made a mistake."

Mom shook her head. "I talked to the social worker, too. She checked the files."

"She doesn't know what she's talking about!" I pounded my fist against the fridge. Magnets and papers went flying.

"No, honey. We got you earlier than expected because the agency honored your birth mother's wish. And the social worker told me that in all likelihood your mother didn't live in Pusan like Hea. She said it was common for mothers from surrounding villages to leave their babies in the city."

"You *wanted* this to happen. You didn't want me to know!" I screamed, my whole body quivering.

"No, Joseph! God no!" Mom started crying.

I cried too, heavy, like a dam unleashed. Mom rushed over and put her arms around me, but I pushed her back.

"Leave me alone!" I growled like a wounded dog.

I pushed the patio screen door open and ran out to the backyard. Past Mom's flowers, past Dad's tomato plants, way back to the shade of the willow tree. I sank down into the coolness of the grass, my head between my knees so no one would see my tears. But Mom followed and sat down next to me. She wrapped her arms across my shoulders and patted my back.

I cried so hard I started hiccupping. Mom kept holding me, wiping back my hair and tears with her purple fingernails.

"How could she just dump me like a bag of trash?" I wailed. "I hate her!" And I did. I hated my birth mother and all the real Koreans. All their faces merged into a kaleidoscope of tears and scowls and empty bassinets.

"I'm sure she loved you, Joseph. She probably felt so frightened, being young, unmarried, and pregnant." Mascara ran down her cheeks. "I know she thinks of you all the time, every single day."

"I came so close to finding her."

"I know this feels awful, but even if you don't find your birth mother—or at least not now—you *will* find out more about who you are. And this time your father and I will help. We promise."

The back gate swung open. "Mr. Twistee is coming down the street, Mom! Can we get ice cream?" Sophie shouted. Gina stood next to her with water dripping from her bikini.

I pulled away from Mom.

"Take some coins from the lunch money jar and leave

us alone," Mom said firmly.

"Why's Joseph crying?" Gina asked.

I didn't stick around for the answer. I leaped toward the house. As I passed Mom's flowers, I pointed at Saint Joseph's concrete chin.

"It's all your fault!" I shouted.

"Phone, Joseph!" Gina yelled outside my bedroom door, later that evening.

"Go away."

"But it's a girl. You always talk when girls call."

"I don't care if it's a supermodel. Buzz off."

Close to dinnertime came another knock. "Come eat something, sweetie," Mom said softly.

I kept the door locked and my eyes staring up at Pegasus on the ceiling, though it was harder to make out the stars during daytime.

Finally I dozed off. When I woke, my Spidey clock flashed 7:52. The sun was setting, and I heard two fists banging from the hallway.

"You gotta let us in, Joseph," Gina pleaded. "We've got three ice-cream sandwiches and a can of root beer we snuck out of the kitchen while Mommy and Daddy went for a walk. If they come home and catch us up here with this stuff, we're dead meat."

"And the ice cream is melting!" Sophie added.

I let them in. They wouldn't care that I had puffy red eyes.

The three of us sat by the foot of my bed in silence, eating drippy ice-cream sandwiches and taking turns gulping the soda. I took a long sip and passed the root beer to Sophie.

"Aren't you going to say, 'No backwash' like you always do?" she asked.

I shook my head. I still wasn't up for talking.

"It's because he's got hurt feelings," Gina said, patting me on the arm with her sticky fingers. "Mom told us everything."

"Told you what?"

"About your birth mother being missing."

"She's not missing, Gina. It's more like she's hiding." Why was I discussing this with two clueless second graders?

"That makes us really mad!" Sophie shouted.

"Why are *you* guys mad?"

"Your birth mother is *not* nice!" Gina agreed, her eyes narrowing behind her glasses. "She's wicked like the evil queen in *Snow White*."

"No, she's not. You just don't get it." I shook my head, but for some strange reason, I suddenly felt a little better.

"Joseph's right, Gina. We shouldn't be mad at his birth mother. I'm glad she let Mommy and Daddy have him because otherwise he wouldn't be in the same family. He wouldn't be our brother." Sophie flashed those big brown eyes of hers. She looked so innocent that I felt guilty for all the times I swore she was possessed.

Gina licked her fingers. "You're wrong, Sophie. Joseph would always be our brother. It's just his birth mother would be our mom."

"Then who would Mommy be?" Sophie asked, totally confused.

"She'd be your hairdresser," I said, fighting back a laugh.

The Three-Eyed Alien

We had a sub in English the next day who let us talk, but I was in no mood for chitchat. Especially with all the jabbering about who was going with who to the dumb dance. Like I cared about eating chicken wings in that stinky gym with a tie on. I mean, I was happy for Nash; Ok-hee had said yes. And her parents were okay with it too—in part because Nash was friends with *me*, so they figured he wasn't a serial killer or anything. But hearing the rest of the eighth-grade lovebirds annoyed me. Then I overheard Jackie Tozzi say that Kelly was going to the Farewell

Formal with Lewis Knight, and that did it. I finished my worksheet, got a pass, and escaped to the library.

"Hey, Joseph!"

I peeked in the gym as I passed, only to see Yongsu waving at me and bouncing a Hacky Sack next to Whitney Bailey. That was a surprise. We call her the Wordless Word Queen because she won the state spelling bee twice, but other than that she barely opens her mouth. Yet there she was, giggling away with Yongsu.

At least someone felt happy.

I walked to the back of the library and searched through the stacks of old *Mad* magazines. They usually cheer me up, even on the darkest day. Finally I found one from two years ago that I hadn't read yet.

"I've been waiting for you," a throaty voice growled from behind me.

I jumped, turned around, and nearly fell back into the shelves. A three-eyed alien glared at me!

Then a hand with half-moon fingernails pulled off the mask. "Gotcha!" Robyn laughed so hard she dropped her alligator mini-pack.

I stood up and shook my head. "Yeah, you got me" was all I could say. But then I cracked up, too. Why is it that getting scared-to-death actually feels hilarious after-ward?

"Serves you right. Don't you return phone calls?" she asked. She was wearing paper clip earrings and her hair was pulled back into a braid with loose strands sticking out the sides.

Whoops. I remembered Gina telling me about a phone call. "Sorry, I didn't know it was you. And I went to sleep early."

We stood there snatching glimpses of each other while pretending we were looking around the library. Robyn began saying something, stopped, and started again. A librarian wheeled a cart of books by. She noticed the mask in Robyn's hand, and smiled.

"I was talking to your friend Pete Nash the other day. I didn't know you read comic books. So do I." Her voice was almost a whisper.

"*Read* 'em? I could be president of the Spidey Fan Club," I said. "I know everything about Spider-Man, from which superhero he met on Christmas Day to Peter Parker and Mary Jane's special love song."

Robyn looked like she was about to burst. "He met The Human Torch and, duh, their song was 'Kung Fu Fighting!' Spider-Man rocks, but Storm's *my* girl. She who controls the weather, controls the world."

"I never knew that you liked comic books, Robyn."

"I bet there's a lot we don't know about each other."

Here was my chance. Yoda's words echoed in my head: *There is no try.*

"Robyn, would you go to the Farewell Formal? With me, I mean?"

"I would, but—"

She stopped. Here we go again. Rejection City, two days straight. Maybe God was punishing me for saying I hated my birth mother.

"Don't even say it Robyn. I understand." Why not spare us both the painful details of her excuse.

"Say what?" She looked hurt.

"Whatever you're going to say to let me down easy." I tossed the *Mad* magazine back on the stack.

Robyn pouted her lips. Her face wasn't as furious as the three-eyed alien's, but it wasn't warm and fuzzy, either.

"So you're making up my mind for me? Is that how it works, Joseph?"

Now I felt like the president of Idiots-R-Us. "No, I misunderstood. I mean . . . what *do* you mean?"

"I was about to say I'll go with you, but not because you're funny. You *are* funny, but not funny looking. You're kind of cute, if you must know." She folded up the mask and stuck it in her mini-pack.

"Really? I mean, thanks," I said. How did she know about my humor dilemma? Nash must have said something to her. And whatever he said had helped, because she was going to the dance with me!

"Did you really think I looked put together last week in study hall?" she asked as we walked toward the front of the library.

"Very put together," I said. I just knew my face was reddening from my goofy attempt to sound like a ladies' man.

We cut across a line of sixth graders checking out books at the circulation counter. I told her I'd buy our dance tickets tomorrow during lunch, since the dance was Friday. Nothing like waiting until last minute.

"Sure," she said, distracted. Then she grabbed my arm—not exactly a yank, but firm enough—and pulled me into the side room where the microfiche viewers are kept.

Our faces were inches away from each other, so close I could count her eyelashes. I half expected her to tell me a dumb riddle, but she didn't say a word.

Instead, she grabbed my chin and kissed me.

"That was no joke," she said. And she strolled away, the alligator tail on her mini-pack bopping up and down behind her, leaving me standing in the library as limp as a rubber band.

I walked into Spanish, my last period class, feeling higher than the world's tallest man on stilts. Happier than a dog with a T-bone. I was the luckiest guy in Nutley, New Jersey. Robyn and I would have a blast at the Farewell Formal. Not that I had to daydream about her or anything, since she was sitting three desks over.

After class I was still in a daze and nearly ran into Mrs. Peroutka in the hallway. She asked if I'd come to her classroom.

I followed her, and she pulled a paper out of a folder. "Here's your makeup essay, Joseph. I wanted to talk about it privately."

Privately? Did that mean more trouble? My eyes zeroed in on the top of the first page. All I saw was a big fat A.

Yowza!

"Thanks," I said, reaching out to shake her hand.

"Describing yourself as an ethnic sandwich was funny and honest, Joseph. You seem to understand your layers better than most people."

"I'm trying," I said, shrugging.

"And I would agree that being adopted, as you wrote,

must raise a 'boatload of questions that don't have easy answers.' You've shown insight that, for some, takes a lifetime to discover."

Mrs. Peroutka was spreading the compliments so thick I felt bad for all the times I'd slept in her class. I vowed never to doze off in social studies again—at least not in the remaining two weeks.

Just as I charged out of the room so I wouldn't miss the bus, Mrs. Peroutka called me back.

"One more thing, Joseph. I'd like to display your essay on the bulletin board, if you're okay with that. The unit is over, but I think your classmates would enjoy reading what you wrote."

"Sure."

"Your writing showed courage and honesty. Even Sohn Kee Chung would be pleased," she added with a smile.

"Hey, Mrs. Nash, is Pete home?" I shouted from the driveway after school. He hadn't been on the bus, and I really wanted to talk to him.

Mrs. Nash was watering the flowerpots on her front stoop. She was still dressed in her nurse's uniform. "He's out back, cleaning the pool."

I unlocked the gate. "What's up, bro?" I called.

"I've got strange but true news, Joseph," he said with a grin.

"What, did Frankie get a date for the dance?"

"Believe it or not, he did. Molly Palanski said yes on a dare, poor girl. But that's not it."

"I give up."

He was grinning. "I just got back from a doctor's appointment. I cracked the case of what's causing my migraines. Even my neurologist thinks I'm right."

"What is it then?"

"Potatoes! Plain old potatoes. Can you believe it?"

I thought about all the gallons of mashed potatoes that he'd eaten over the years. I could only imagine his mom's shock at the news.

"Talk about a cruel twist of fate," I said. "But it could have been worse. What if you'd been allergic to candy?"

Nash said he was registered for summer baseball for the first time in two years. "And I might even be able to play hockey next year if I lay off the taters."

"Awesome! I've got news too. You and Ok-hee better save room on the dance floor for Robyn and me." I jumped on the picnic table and started doing my best macarena moves.

"You won her over?" Nash's eyes twinkled.

"Yup. And I didn't use one single joke," I said, patting my own back. "I owe you, too, man. For talking me up with Robyn."

"Both our dates were collaborative efforts," Nash said, using a deep spy voice.

"Never use that word 'collaborative.' It's too teacher-ish," I said, and we both laughed.

Nash said that he and Ok-hee would be riding to the dance with her brother. "You'll never believe who Yongsu's taking," he said.

"Whitney the Wordless Word Queen?"

He nodded. "Did he tell you?"

"Just a hunch. Yongsu didn't say a word. And we both know Whitney's a good speller but a lousy talker!"

Nash finished cleaning the pool and tossed the skimmer on the grass. "Want to swim?"

"Sure," I said. Nash belly flopped in and I followed, causing a tidal wave that drenched the picnic table.

I was wearing jean shorts, but I didn't care. In fact, we made so much noise acting like caffeinated dolphins that Mrs. Nash came out and offered us snacks just to get us out of the water.

Close to dinnertime, I dried off and put on my sneakers.

Nash crossed his arms over his chest, hesitated, and then spoke. "I'm sorry about the search, Joseph. That it didn't work out."

I shrugged. "It's not your fault, Nash. The odds weren't with us that the right person would read my posting."

To use Mom-speak, I'd taken a chill pill. I wasn't even mad at my birth mother anymore, whatever her name is. I mean, it's not like I got shipped to Slumsville, USA.

"It's up to you, Joseph. But if you want to keep searching, well, I'm here and I charge reasonable rates."

I smiled and told Nash I'd keep that in mind.

As I walked up my driveway in my dripping wet shorts, I figured out why I've always loved Spider-Man. Throughout his whole life Peter Parker tried, but never uncovered, what happened after his parents disappeared behind the Iron Curtain as spies. It always bugged him that he couldn't get to the truth, and, yeah, a couple of times he followed false leads, thinking he'd found his parents when he hadn't. Still, it didn't stop him from being the coolest. Even better than Superman, if you ask me. Sure, Superman is invincible—nothing but a wad of kryptonite can take him out. But Spider-Man, well, he started out human like the rest of us. And he rights the world using his web slinging and wisecracking.

Besides, my birth mother didn't go behind the Iron Curtain. She probably never even left her village in Korea. Someday I might find her. And this time I'll be sure to ask what religion she is *first*.

Why Not Both?

"Don't drop those Whoppers," Dad called that evening as I followed him to a table in the back of Burger King, where Mom was waiting with Gina and Sophie. Since Dad still had his cast on, I was the designated carrier. And this was the mother of all fast-food trays, piled high with supersized drinks, burgers, fries, and lots of ketchup in paper cups.

"Where's my fish fillet?" Sophie asked, scanning the wrapped burgers.

Mom dug it out from under the pile and passed it to her.

I looked at Sophie's sandwich and grasped at my chest. "How dare you eat a fish that was so cruelly hooked, skinned, and fried!"

"Not funny, Joseph. And neither is killing cow mothers in front of their puppies."

"Calves, Sophie," Dad said, biting into his burger. "If you're going to be an animal rights activist, at least get the names straight."

Sophie was still on her animal cruelty kick. Was she a born-again vegan or was this a passing second-grade fad? Only time would tell. Time and Mom's risotto and sausage, which so happened to be Sophie's favorite meal.

After they'd finished, Sophie and Gina ran over to play on the indoor jungle gym. I got up to get more ketchup. Like Dad, I use tons of the stuff.

"By the way, Joseph. Nonna and Nonno Calderaro are flying up next week for your moving-up ceremony," Mom said.

"Great! We haven't seen them since Christmas," I said.

Dad sipped his shake. "Nonno wouldn't miss your last drum solo in middle school. He bought himself a digital camera so he could e-mail your picture to all his golf buddies in Florida. Don't be surprised if he makes copies of your report card and that terrific essay to show off too. Those old fellows like to one-up each other."

"Ah yes, Competitive Grandparents Duke it Out in Florida. Now *that's* a reality show," I said, drumming my fingertips against the edge of the table.

Dad laughed. "Nonno's proud of you, Joseph; we all are. What a way to end the year: a band solo and high honors for your grades. High school will suit you well."

"Speaking of suits, I permed Donnalee Carleton's hair this afternoon," Mom said.

I gulped down a mouthful of fries. "As in Robyn's mother?" Guess Mom knows who I'm taking to the Farewell Formal on Friday!

"Robyn's grandmother."

"I meant to tell you that I asked Robyn to the dance, Mom. It just happened today."

"Don't worry, I knew before my two o'clock appointment showed up. Robyn called Mrs. Carleton from the school pay phone, and her mother called Donnalee on her cell phone while she was sitting under the dryer. The Carletons are nice people. Donnalee's a great tipper, too."

Dad winked at me. "See? You were yourself and you got the girl."

"Yup, I let my true colors show. Like Caruso."

"How 'bout we go to the mall after school tomorrow and get you a suit?" Dad asked.

"Works for me," I said, with my mouth full.

"Get a dark color," Mom added. "The way things are going with Aunt Foxy and Dominick, you might need it for a winter wedding."

I nodded. "Dominick can marry Aunt Foxy as long as he gets me tickets to a Yankees game."

"Gets us *both* tickets," Dad said, and I high-fived his good arm.

I grabbed a handful of Mom's fries, and she pushed the rest over to me.

"I was telling Mom that I checked out the college library today," Dad said.

Dad likes libraries as much as I like comic book stores, so that was nothing new.

"And while I was there, I did some research on Korea and adoption searching," he added.

I stopped chewing.

"Turns out they offer these group tours, for families and adoptees wanting to visit their birthplace."

I started chewing again, but quietly, so I wouldn't miss a word.

"The tour groups don't guarantee they can reunite

adoptees with birth families, but they can connect us with Korean agencies that do these kinds of searches. Korea used to be close-lipped about this stuff, but that's changing."

"So we'll go to Pusan?" I asked. Whoa, was this my dad or an alien impostor?

"That's right. We'll do our best to track down your birth relatives, and we'll see the city you're from."

"With other adopted kids?"

"Sure, kids and their families. These tours aren't cheap, but I'm thinking we'll go the summer before your junior year. That's only two years out, and by then I'll be halfway done with my bachelor degree and ready for a vacation. Just think, you and me—Pusan bound," he said, grinning.

In my whole life, Dad and I never traveled anywhere together, just us.

"Count me in." I looked over at Mom. Her eyes sparkled in a way that said it all: *See, Joseph, he does care.*

"You're in, son. Start saving your allowance for kimchi dinners. I read that Koreans have their own version of calamari, too." Dad snatched some of Mom's fries from my pile.

He remembered about kimchi. We'd love kimchi and calamari!

"Before you two jet-setters book airfare, I want dates and times so I can check the astrology charts," she said. "Laugh all you want, but no way are you flying on a bad day for a Taurus or a Scorpio."

My déjà-vu dream returned that night. Only this time, there was a guest star. A man running up ahead on the dirt road slowed down and called me. "Joseph!"

I stared at him. Finally a face that *wasn't* fuzzy. It was Sohn Kee Chung!

"Good work," he said, jogging in place beside me now and gesturing toward my wagon. "You're almost there. Keep pulling."

"But where am I going?" I asked.

The sunlight flickered against something around his neck. His gold medal. "Where do you want to go?" he asked.

I shrugged, confused.

"Pusan is waiting for you, Joseph. Naples and Florence, too. You don't want to miss any of it. I'm glad I went to Germany."

"But . . ."

"Happy traveling, Joseph," he said, patting my back before he took off again.

"Thanks, Sohn . . . Grandpa," I called in the faintest whisper.

A small brown package came addressed to me in the mail on the day of the Farewell Formal. Mom was out running errands when I opened it. The St. Louis return address gave it away: I didn't know anyone who lived there but Jae.

Inside was a small envelope, wrapped in bubble wrap, and a letter written on flowery stationery.

> Dear Joseph,
>
> I know we're not blood related, but I haven't been able to let you go. The thought of being your cousin brought me great joy.
>
> It's a Korean tradition for parents to have a dojang made when a child is born. A dojang is a rubber stamp using Chinese characters that represent your name. Chinese characters are often used on important documents when a signature is needed. Dojangs are used to sign official letters.
>
> We have a small Korean shop here in St. Louis, and I ordered this one with your name.

Did you know Duk-kee means "virtue" and "profit"? A perfect Korean name for a young man I have come to admire.

Use your dojang proudly, Joseph. And know that being Korean isn't something you have to prove. You are as real Korean as you can be.

Fondly,

Jae

I held the *dojang* by its smooth wooden handle, and my fingers touched the ridges in the rubber mat.

This is my name. What my birth mother called me. I thought back to that wave of joy that hit when I first learned about Jae's aunt. I really believed I'd found my birth mother.

I sighed. Then I said my Korean name out loud.

"Duk-kee."

And for the first time, it sounded just the way Yongsu said it!

I carried the *dojang* upstairs to my room. My suit was already laid out on my bed. Dad had polished my black leather shoes and pre-knotted my tie. And Mom had picked up a wrist corsage for Robyn, which was sitting on my dresser.

Just before I took a shower, I reached behind my bed and picked up the *corno* box.

I unclasped the chain and put it around my neck. Just like Dad and Nonno Calderaro and Uncle Biaggio, I was as real Italian as I could be too.

I'd wear the *corno* to the dance. And I'd use the *dojang* whenever I needed to sign my name in a fancy way. Maybe I'd bring it to the Jiffy Wash to show Mrs. Han, especially now that I could say my name like a real Korean.

Why not do both? There are worse things than being an ethnic sandwich.

Special Thanks

It takes a village to raise a children's book, too. Family, friends, fellow writers, children, teachers, librarians, and adoption advocates have left their imprint on my story. I am grateful to you all.

My parents, Theresa and Harry Kent, whose love and commitment teach me everything I need to know about creating the story of a good life

My four superkids: TJ, wise teen editor and comic book connoisseur; Kellyrose, my sounding board who made sure I "wrote it real"; Connor, the original Buddha Baby; and Theresa, the cutest cheerleader I could have on my team

Patricia Reilly Giff, mentor and friend whose "You will publish" words echoed through the dark

Jae Kim, my Yale angel who enlightened me on Korea's proud history

Young-jung Yoon, who filled in the cultural blanks and patiently educated me on Korean ways

Rachel Orr, savvy editor extraordinaire, for following "the signs" and believing in a boy named Joseph

Writers on Wednesday Nancy Castaldo, Liza Frenette, Lois Miner Huey, Coleen Paratore, and Kyra Teis. You are the best writers group on this side of the Hudson River. And another book with our word in it, WOW!

Tom Henery, who answered every band question I could e-throw at him. Go Navy!

Jennifer Groff, literary goddess, whose passion for children's books inspires me

Sal Primeggia, for Italian historical perspective; Sandy Dagliolo, for Italian translation; Abby Curro, for her calamari recipe; Jeanie Orr, for insight on the dojang; Ben Falge at the Japanese Connection, for the beautiful dojang *artwork; Jean and Tom Spiegelhalter, for "showing me" St. Louis; Virginia Horn and Barbara Restivo, for constant encouragement; Michelle Camuglia, my first local reader; and Laura Garrity, for the New Jersey geography lesson*

Finally, to the many caring birth mothers, adoptees, and adoptive parents who graciously shared their stories, sometimes with teary eyes. I am blessed to have heard it all

And to Tom, who opened the windows and let the fresh air in.